I0783706

Millones Cajones

Rob Bell

BackHouse Books
California

Also from BackHouse Books

Where'd You Park Your Spaceship?
Book 1: Welcome to Firdus

Where'd You Park Your Spaceship?
Book 2: There's Only One Noon Yeah

What's a Knucka?
A play

We'll Get Back to You
A play

R

Seriously, you would think by now I wouldn't tear up, but I do —every time. It's not that it isn't a good story, it's just that I've heard it so many times—wait, I think, yes, I actually have the hard data written down here.

I've heard it 73 times.

And now, right now, I am ashamed to admit that I just did that thing where you inhale really fast through your nose so that you won't have to blow it because I actually felt a tear forming from hearing this story for the 73rd time. I could tell the story. I could give the whole talk. Only being the sap I am, I'd , probably choke up at this point.

This point being an hour and six minutes in—he times things to the minute—and with only seven minutes to go it's what he calls the "DM" for the talk. That means defining moment. He insists there's a point when people are hearing something meaningful that they make subconscious decisions affecting the rest of their lives. They know they're moved and inspired and changed by what they're hearing, but he's convinced these DMs open windows of time when the subterranean forces just below the surface of our psyche actually steer the ship of our actions and we're never the same—or something like that.

Anyway, he says this story is the DM of this talk. Right now he's telling the part about this Peruvian girl who lives on one side of a mountain in...uh, Peru...and someone—maybe her sister but it might be her aunt or teacher—is sick and actually everybody in her village is sick. But they've heard that in the village on the other side of the mountain is a doctor who has medicine that will make them all well. So this girl announces she's going over the mountain to get the medicine, but everybody protests and says she's too young, and she won't know how to navigate the jungle and she'll get eaten by hyenas.

Which I swear is a detail he added because everyone knows hyenas don't live in Peru, although as I'm saying this so confidently I'm realizing maybe I'm wrong and have no idea what I'm talking about. He does this all the time, adding all sorts of details to his stories that are easy to pass right over until you actually think about them for a second. Like this one story he told in his first book about the ship's captain who developed a rash that was so bad it turned a burnt green color (burnt green?). Or he used to tell this other story about a football team, and he'd always mention how the players "folded their socks over three times at the knees."

We were all talking about this one time because Noll brought up how our boss always describes his mentor as having the kind of eyebrows "you'd see in a museum," and we were all like "What the...?" So now if we're all standing in the back while he's speaking when he throws in these random details, we just smile at each other knowingly because everyone in the entire audience just sits there and takes it, as if it's the most normal thing in the world to hear a man's eyebrow's described as the kind you'd find in a museum.

Back to the girl in Peru...so the whole village eventually realizes she's their only hope, and if she doesn't make this journey they're all going to die and so they gather around her as she's packing up her donkey and the village elders say a blessing over her and they give her the traditional Peruvian kiss on the forehead and then one of the oldest women in the village says, "Make sure you strap that ass tight!"

And the crowd erupts. Like they always do. That line kills them. He talks quietly and slowly up to this point, whether we're in Toledo or Dallas or Syracuse, and you can always hear a pin drop as he gets more and more somber and serious painting this picture of the villagers gathered around this girl

who's packing up her donkey. And then he does the "strap
your ass tight" line, and they're caught off guard and
absolutely lose it. In Jacksonville three weeks ago, I was
watching a large man in plaid shorts sitting on the end of the
aisle and he was so into the story that when that line dropped
he actually fell off his chair into the aisle. Swear to you. It
happened...

Y

These are the moments I live for.

I'll take the weight and responsibility and pressure and all that
comes with it for those killer moments when it's just me and
the crowd, and I get to deliver a line like "strap your ass tight"
and the whole time I know what's coming. I'm talking softer
and slower as I stretch out the drama of the girl getting ready
to leave the village. There is a particular stillness in the room.
It's one of the few moments in my life when all is calm and I'm
at peace. I often think at this point, "I've got them right where I
want them," and then I deliver the line and the room explodes.

Sometimes I pause an extra millisecond just to savor the
moment before I say the line. It's such a rush— I'd love to
know if there is some sort of machine that could monitor my
body in such a moment because my blood even feels different,

like I'm floating. And I've done this talk so many times— how many now? Fifty? A hundred?

Rooster will know. He always knows the "hard data" as he calls it. I remember the first time he used that phrase "hard data" with a straight face. Really, hard data? Who talks like that? I reminded him people don't care about hard data; they want stories. They want inspiration. They want relief. They want to know they can be great.

That's what I do. I get paid to tell people they can be great.

R

Once the crowd has settled down and stopped laughing and they collect themselves, Yves delivers the knockout line. Yes, Yves—did I forget to tell you his name? It's pronounced "V," as in the letter, not "eaves," like the overhang of your roof, which is how some people try to pronounce it. He says it's because his mom lived in Paris once and worked for Yves St. Laurent or something like that... so after the girl packs up her donkey, or tightens her ass as the case would be, and the villagers say a blessing over her blah blah blah, she walks up the trail and out of sight as everyone stares in silent amazement. Then one of the young villagers turns to his brother and says, "That girl has millones cajones." As in million-dollar testicles. I'll bet Yves has made a million dollars off that line. People absolutely love

it. They remember it. They write it in marker on their arms.
They buy the shirts with the MC logo on it, they buy the visor
and the key chain and the book and the music CD and the
study guide and the duffel bag and the beach chair. I'm not
exaggerating. For a while we sold a Millones Cajones beach
chair. How desperate is that? And when I told Yves and Noll
we were selling way too much crap, and it might seem, well,
desperate to cash in on the popularity of the phrase, Yves
immediately responded, "Not as desperate as the person who
hasn't experienced their own greatness."

Which is what he often does.

He comes back at you so quickly with something sounding so
profound you don't know what to say so you say nothing
because you don't want to appear slow. But you suspect he's
just talking bollocks, but it may of course be really deep... and
then after the girl leaves her village and Yves does the
"millones cajones" bit, he tells a series of stories quickly, one
right after one another.

The first one is about a guy interviewing for a job and it looks
like he's going to get it, but there's intense competition for the
position. So at the end of the meeting the guy takes a sheet of
paper and writes some numbers on it and slides it across the
table to his interviewers and says, "I won't take the job for less
than this number in salary and bonuses." The interviewers look

at one another and then offer him the job. I know it sounds really bold and cocky and arrogant, but when Yves tells the story it somehow becomes really inspiring, the kind of thing everybody wishes they had the guts, excuse me, the millones cajones, to pull off.

And then Yves tells about the owner of a company who heard that two of his executives in an office on the other side of the country weren't getting along so the CEO got on a plane and several hours later walked into their office, demanding a meeting to get everything out in the open. His two execs were stunned that their boss valued them enough to travel across the country just to resolve their conflict, and almost immediately the three of them were laughing about it and planning their company's next big merger.

And then Yves tells about a public school teacher whose principal wouldn't let her experiment with some new classroom ideas on how to engage the kids and told her to "keep your newfangled ideas about education to yourself." And so just to show him up, she stopped talking and from then on only taught her class using sign language, which in no time meant her entire class learned sign language, and then their test scores went up and she won all sorts of awards. When the press came to the school, they interviewed the principal who pretended like her teaching method was all his idea, but then when they tried to interview her, she gave all her answers in sign language. Because the principal couldn't interpret what she was saying on camera, it became clear he had been trying to take the credit for something he had no idea about. She showed that principal a thing or two about what it means to have—say it with me now—"Millones Cajones!"

Now I know what you're thinking. That the whole cojones theme kind of crumbles when the examples in Yves' stories are women. But that's my point—when he tells it, it works. People look past such obvious details as women and cojones, and the relationship thereof, and any notions about it sounding sexist, because of the sheer force of his personality. Or maybe it's because he just goes for it without any sense of apology or intentional offense. I've heard people describe his appeal for years now, from the brilliant to the stupid (One reporter in a radio interview wondered aloud, on the air, if it was Yves' French name that makes people like him before they've ever even heard him speak. The interviewer referred to it as a "linguistic presumptive disposition," which seemed like the most pretentious NPR kind of phrase to drop until the guy concluded, "Just imagine if Yves' name was Lionel, or Horace, or Milford" which made me think again).

So Yves tells all of these stories about people who have millones cajones, which build toward a crescendo about how these kinds of people do the courageous, risky thing no matter how tough it is and regardless of how great the risk is and no matter how many hyenas are lurking in the jungle. (See, now you get how corny it is, but it works, I swear to you, it works. People eat this stuff up— even if they know there aren't hyenas in Peru.)

Then he asks, "What's on the other side of your mountain? What do you know you must do, no matter what it may cost you or how long it may take?"

It's really quiet then (remember, this is a DM) because people are thinking long and hard about their lives and their dreams and their goals, and after pausing Yves finishes by shouting, "So strap that ass tight and get going!"

And they jump to their feet and start cheering and clapping and doing what people do at motivational seminars when they've been rescued for a few moments from their dull, uninspired lives...

It happens like this every time. I've seen this very scene unfold live in person 73 times. People just go crazy. One time, I believe it was in Tulsa, I actually saw grown men and women form a conga line—that awkward dance thing where you put your hands on the shoulders in front of you and dance/walk/waddle—only in this case they all ended up standing in a line trying to figure out where to go and how to dance and keep the hysteria alive with their hands on each other's shoulders. Painful to watch, just painful.

Y

A few more waves, a few more high fives with people in the front row, a few more fist bumps and then I am off the stage. What a feeling. There's this interesting detail I've been noticing lately, the weight of my feet on the stairs leading off the stage right after I've spoken. Strange the sensations you become aware of when you've been doing something this long. There is a particular feeling when I'm walking up onto the stage in which I become acutely aware of how my feet feel in my socks and the insoles of my shoes and the bottoms of my feet sinking into the tops of the stairs. It's as if I can feel all of the tension and excitement and anticipation of what's about to happen—in my feet. And then when I walk off, the same exact feet touch the same exact stairs but everything is totally different. Relief. Lightness of being. Release. Sometimes it feels like I'm floating off the stage, barely touching the stairs. I once sat next to a yoga instructor (he referred to himself as a yogi! Please!) on an airplane, and he was talking about chakras and energy fields and the transference of the earth's magnetic polarity, and it all sounded like such rubbish at the time. But I swear something is going on with those stairs.

R

And now I'm walking...because when duty calls I always answer. He's standing on stage waving and shaking hands with people in the front row, and I need to be backstage in about two minutes to do "the ritual," as we call it: one minute for him to grab a water (He times everything to the minute— everything.); one minute for us to discuss how the talk went. Which usually goes something like this:

Yves: "Were they pumped up or what?"
Me: "Oh, they were pumped up all right!"
Yves: "What a crowd!"
Me: "Now that was a crowd…"

And then he asks how long the line is for his book signing. The truth is I never know because it hasn't formed yet, and if it has formed, I'm back here, of course, with him so how would I know?

Besides, is he actually listening? Does he really want to know? Would he not go out there if some minimum number of people were not lined up to his liking? And while I'm getting some things off my chest, we never actually critique the talk, do we? Because would he actually change the talk after the 73rd time? Would he suddenly realize, "Hey, that thing I say at minute 23 makes no sense!" I don't think so. As you can see, I have questions about the relevancy of the ritual...sometimes I throw in all sorts of details just to see if he's listening. "Oh yeah, the signing line is long, it goes past the bar where they serve those little pretzels with that funky chili powder salt on them and then around the corner where the women's restroom is and then down the hall with the maroon carpet with yellow trim and into the lobby that has the giant gold statue of a flamingo in the fountain that sounds exactly like someone peeing…"

Y

One minute for water. Another minute for PGD. That's post game debrief. It's absolutely critical that I continue to improve everything I'm doing. So right after I leave the stage, Rooster and I spend a minute evaluating how the talk went, the strengths and weaknesses. I'm always looking for that one detail that could be changed to make it even better. Can't rest on what I've done, have to keep raising the bar. That's why I surround myself with people like Rooster, people who are totally committed to what I'm doing and willing to make the kind of sacrifices required to pull this off. He's been with me for what, seven years now?

R

So the ritual is done, or PGD as he calls it, and it's time to move. Where is Noll? He's usually here by now. I give Yves a basic idea about where we're headed and out of the dressing room we go...

Y

God, I need a chair. Now. There's one. Almost. Yes…good. Sitting down. What's going on with me? A headache? Vertigo? I want Rooster to stop talking. Get that hand up to make him stop. There. My hand is now up. What is this? Why does everything feel slow and heavy like the air's been coated with lead? Words sound like marbles rattling in my ears. Just need a minute to clear things out, conquer this. Whatever it is.

R

Something's up. He's stopped and he just sat down. "Yves, what's going on?" No response. Just a hand held up with that universal gesture of "Give me a minute." So I stand here, in the bowels of a convention center. In a long hall with white walls and shiny tile floor and laundry bins along the wall and an exit sign several hundred feet away. Two minutes late in hustling the great Yves Green, motivational speaker, to his table in the lobby to sign books. This has never happened before.

N

What the hell? I come around the corner and Rooster is in full ritual mode with his ever-present clipboard (For someone who claims he's so technologically progressive, why does he carry that old school brown clipboard with him? My sergeant carried one of those...thirty years ago.), and Yves is sitting in one of those metal folding chairs just past the delivery entrance behind the stage staring straight ahead. I look at Rooster and he gives me that "whatever you're missing, I'm missing, too" look. And so I just stand there. And Rooster just stands there. And Yves sits there. Awkward, this.

R

Noll comes around the corner, sees Yves sitting down staring straight ahead, and looks at me with that "Am I missing something?" look. I start to ask Yves again, and he holds up his hand again.

N

So do I say something? What? I've been in countless weird situations with Yves before but never one where he was just sitting there doing nothing and not saying anything. Enough of this, I clap my hands and bark, "We got books to sell, boss!"

R

Classic Noll. "We got books to sell, boss!" Only Noll would do that. Then again, only Noll calls Yves "Boss" to his face and gets away with it. Yves actually loves it.

Y

Books? Yes, books. Books to sell. Whatever that was it's gone. For a moment I had no energy— not the tired, drowsy, need-more-sleep kind of no-energy, but some sort of all over my body no-energy that made it almost impossible to walk. But now I'm fine. So here we go, time to meet my fans...

N

Whatever that was, he seems fine now, so true to the ritual, he's going to need directions: "On the other side of these doors is a big column, we'll turn right at it and go past the elevators to the atrium—we've got most of it roped off, but we'll go across the hall and the desk is right there. Ron from B&N is heading up point."

R

A bit about Noll. He's six foot four, not an ounce of body fat, solid muscle, with a flat top haircut (or maybe it's a crew cut-or is that a brush cut-what is the difference?). He's at least sixty years old, and his clothes are perfect. Not a spot on them. Totally pressed all the time. No matter where we are, no matter how far we've travelled, he always looks like he walked out of a catalogue. One time in Missoula, Yves was doing a talk for the National Rodeo Association Rider of the Year Awards Banquet (no comment) and Noll shows up in blue jeans with a crease down the front! Do you know anybody who irons their jeans? He wears a silver ring on the pinky finger of his right hand that has an eagle on it and he's always, always wearing Birkenstock sandals. Snowing and sleeting? Birkenstocks. A sizzling 120 degrees in Palm Springs? Birkenstocks. Sometimes with bare feet, and sometimes with colored socks with stripes on them.

One time I asked him why he only wears sandals. He paused, took a deep breath, crossed his legs, and answered: "In Vietnam, we had to wear boots, every day, all the time, wherever we went. And I hated those damn boots. They'd get water in them and then my feet would sweat and then we'd hike for miles and then they'd dry out and then we'd wade through another swamp and then we'd go to sleep still wearing them and then we'd wake up with itching feet but we'd have to immediately start walking in them..." So I made a vow that if I got home alive, I would never wear uncomfortable shoes again as long as I lived. So Rooster, my good man, these aren't just sandals, these are a daily celebration of my American freedom. I'm so glad you asked."

I trust you're getting a sense of Noll. But there's one more detail you need to know: Noll has a mustache, and not just a "mustache" mustache, but he has one with handles on the ends, waxed into shape daily by the owner of said mustache.

Once again, that's Noll. Big, strong, fancy mustached man in pressed pants, colored socks and sandals who runs the merch table for a motivational speaker whose first name is Yves. It's not an easy job selling over priced t-shirts and plaques with sayings on them about "character" and "risk" and "perseverance" that inspire you for a while until you realize you're still the same schmuck you've always been. But Noll can move the merch. He runs the table and now web store. ("Cross promotional synergy, Rooster, it's the future!")

One more story about Noll. We were loading the van one time in Philadelphia, I think it was on South street, and it was late at night, when this man in a hooded jacket appears out of nowhere, pulls out a knife, holds it up to Noll's side and says, "Give me all you got, Flat-top!"

Now up until this point in my life I'd never been involved in any sort of crime whatsoever except when I was in third grade and my babysitter's bike got stolen from our porch. So I'm frozen in place, standing there in this alley late at night watching Noll get mugged, wondering if he might have cash from the merch table stuffed in his jacket pockets because he hasn't had time to lock it away in the safe.

You know what Noll does? He looks this knife wielding midnight killer in the eye and says, "For your information, it's called a crew cut. A flat top, as anyone with even rudimentary knowledge of barbering knows, crops the hair closely on the sides to accentuate the curvature of the skull, whereas the crew cut keeps the sides layered, growing progressively longer until it blends in to the hair on top."

I swear that's word-for-word what Noll said. Yves was there, ask him. Like me, he's frozen in place, but not Noll who's calm as can be. The mugger, however, goes ballistic and starts shaking his knife in Noll's face and yelling something about "the end of the world," or maybe it was "the end of your world." I couldn't quite make it out because Noll spun around, grabbed his wrist, kicked the knife out of the guy's hand, yanked his other hand behind his back, pinned him to the ground, put a knee in his back, pulls his cell phone out of his coat pocket, tosses it to me, and casually says, "Rooster, would you please give the local authorities a call while I keep this gentleman occupied?"

And to answer your question, yes, he was. He was wearing Birkenstocks.

So that's Noll, who at this moment is telling Yves, "Ron from B&N will run point..." as we head through the back hallway and into the lobby. Noll plans Yves' signings like they're military operations, which is so ludicrous sounding at first that you assume he's joking. Do you know what "running point" means at a book signing? It means Ron Somebody from the local B&N bookstore will have an extra Sharpie marker in case the one Yves is using runs out. It means he'll ask each person just before they get to the front of the line who they want their book/poster/piece of crap signed to and then he'll write that on a sticky note and attach it to the book/banner/piece of crap so Yves doesn't have to ask them how to spell their name. That, my friend, is running point.

C

Where are they? They're at least four minutes late. This is a long line and it's getting longer. Noll is never late and Yves is never late and Rooster is Rooster...so where are they?

R

And as we round the corner into the atrium there stands Claudia in all of her Claudia-ness. And Claudia is not pleased. "You're late. What's the problem?"

Y

I am a grown man. I am on the way to becoming a moderately successful motivational speaker. I have no fear of standing all alone on a stage in front of thousands of people. And yet Claudia has the power to reduce me to a stuttering junior high student with a minimum of effort on her part. "Sorry, I got hung up on something."

R

"Hung up on something?" is that what we're calling it? Whatever happened back in that hall was being "Hung up on something?"

Y

I always do signings. After every event. I always have and I always will. It's part of the commitment I've made to my fans. Rooster thinks that signings can get a little weird, but he doesn't understand they're where I get to interact with my people. It's just a moment for me—a signature, a picture, a handshake—it takes me just a minute to let someone know I care for them and it means the world to them. Why would I not do it?

It definitely has a cost, though, like right now. I'm exhausted. And that's a long line. But this is where the great ones reach down deep and call on that extra bit of effort that takes them over the top. I can't tell you how many times I've been absolutely spent after a talk, but I went out there and did the signing anyway. Everyday I reach down and I gut it out and that's why I am where I am today. It's all about how far you're willing to go...

R
Claudia, Claudia, Claudia.

How to describe the impossible convergence of awesomeness that is Claudia? Claudia does all of Yves' public relations. She's the one in charge of making sure Yves leaves what she calls "a trail of inspiration" behind him wherever he goes. I know what you're thinking. You're thinking that "trail of inspiration" is the cheesiest line you've ever heard, just the kind of thing a motivation speaker's PR person would say. And, well, that's true. Let me describe her.

Claudia is large. She calls it "big boned." She's medium height and has short hair that she straightens and then streaks with different colors depending on the time of the year. Yesterday she announced, "Valentine's Day is coming and I've got a surprise cookin' for ya'll!" And she has a really deep voice— the first time I heard her laugh, I thought it was a drive-by. Which kind of make senses, because she's from Flint. Highest crime rate in Michigan. Claudia's tough. Really tough. Her dad built Ford F150 pickups at a plant in Detroit his whole life so she drives one to this day in honor of him. Picture her behind the wheel of one of those giant pick ups—her latest one is gold—not tan, but gold. With mud flaps. And tinted windows. And a vanity plate that reads: "CLDPWR," as in "Claudia Power."

Oh, and did I mention that she's Black? And she never gets tired. And she never forgets even the smallest detail. And she's always early. And—ready for this?—she's married to…Noll.

I know.

It took me a while to get used to it, too. The first month we all worked together I would actually watch to see if they got in the same car and drive off together because I just couldn't picture it. Noll and Claudia, cleaning the house and doing dishes and yard work and paying bills, really? Just couldn't get my mind around them being together in the first place, let alone that marriage working. But now, it seems the most normal thing imaginable. They are absolutely totally devoted to each other —and to Yves. Because this work is our life. Me, Noll, Claudia, and, of course, the man with millones cojones himself, Yves. This is what we do with our lives, and it takes everything we have.

Y

This line is going to take everything I have. Normally I have no problem getting up for the crowds, the line, the pictures, the hugs, the super fans—it all energizes me. Instead of being up there on the stage, I'm right here eye to eye with my people, hearing stories about how I'm actually helping them change their lives. But today. Today is different. And Claudia just said something about the line being longer than expected. I cannot think of a single time I've ever heard "more people than expected" that it didn't send pure adrenaline surging through my body. I love it when people's expectations are blown. They set out a hundred chairs and two hundred people show up. I love that.

R
So Yves is sitting down behind the signing table and Ron has a back up Sharpie in hand and Claudia is at her post and Noll is over at the merch table and I'm sitting just behind Yves and here comes the first person in line. She looks to be in her early fifties and she's got something in her hands, a package of some sort she wants to give Yves. She hands it to him shyly and he opens it and it's a sweater. A handmade sweater. A fire-engine red handknit sweater with little silver stars stitched all over the chest.

She says, "I heard you talk three years ago in Trenton, and you were explaining to us how some people choose to be on fire with life and passion and excitement, and you explained how certain colors have certain psychological effects, and when you were talking about red, I just knew that I was supposed to make you this red sweater."
Yves: "Wowww....yes.....thank you so much... so kind of you..."
Her: "I've been working on it for three years..."
Yves: "Well, that's quite impressive..."

Me (to myself): "Three years! You've been living in New Jersey knitting one sweater for three years for someone you've never met?"

Can you see why I could never do what Yves does? This is the first person in the line, and we've already crossed over into Crazy Land, but you know what he says to her?

"Thank you so much for this gift! How about I put it on and let's have our picture taken together so you have a way to remember this moment." And then before she can respond, he does it. He actually puts the sweater on. The lady is so thrilled she actually tears up. I'm doing all I can not to burst out laughing because the sweater makes Yves look like he's fifty-five and working for the post office and living in his parents' basement playing with his model trains in his spare time. But he loves doing this. I have seen him do this sort of thing for years now. He will stop at nothing to connect with people. He has no shame, and he has no fashion sense, because that is one ill-fitting sweater. I make eye contact with Claudia who is shaking her head with her "Only Yves" look. I take the woman's camera and they pose and then she walks away and Yves turns to me and says, "Amazing—what dedication. " I respond, "Amazing—the fit."

Y

Rooster just doesn't get it. He's as good as they come with the details and logistics, but he doesn't understand what it takes to connect with people. That woman matters, she spent all that time making that sweater, and the least I can do is give her the thrill of putting it on. I bet she'll frame that picture.

R

Next up: a group of forty-something business guys, all of them wearing those cell phone holsters on their belts, sensible khaki pants, and sport coats with no ties. And they are fired up to meet Yves, who one of them calls "the man," as in, "Yves, you are the man. We all took your bootstrap challenge and watch all your videos, and every time you're anywhere close we come hear you."

I should explain here, Yves' first book was Bootstraps, and in the back of the book people could take his "Bootstrap Challenge," which was this year-long program to "pull yourself up and take back control of your life." They're still gushing, "And we just think you're the best—will you sign our programs?"

Yves does. He gives them high fives. They then give each other high fives because they just got high fives from "the man."

They walk away giving each other another round of high fives...

I need to make a confession here. These interactions between Yves and his fans should inspire me. They should be reminders that all the work we're doing is helping people—but it doesn't. If I'm really honest, it depresses me. It just seems sort of desperate...

Y

"Rooster—hey Rooster, can you get me a water?"

R

Yves needs water, which means I'm going to need to head back to the dressing room. Which sounds kind of nice right now, taking a break from the signing line. I should tell you how I got into this in the first place. Maybe before that I should start with the whole name thing. My real name is Donald Paul Sloughshinski, which means as a kid I was called "Donnie." Which was fine until "New Kids on the Block" came out and one of them was named Donnie and then I just had to change it because that group absolutely sucked. And seeing as I was into rap at the time—you know, old school N.W.A. and Public Enemy, the real thing—I decided to change my name to "D." I asked everybody to call me "D." Teachers, parents, friends, I was insistent. No more Donnie, it's D from now on. D is in the house. Which is a bit of a problem when you live in a small town in Ohio and everybody knows your name is really Donald. And the Sloughshinski part? Polish.

In my junior year of high school, I was in a drama class and we each had to pretend to be an animal. I chose to be a wolf because that was the fiercest animal I could think of. So we're all in character, and I'm down on all fours and it's a cacophony of animal noises with everybody doing their thing and I let out the most primal wolf noise I can make but it comes out sounding like a...Rooster. Everybody stops what they're doing and the teacher says "Donnie" — see, the D didn't really stick — "that is the best rooster impersonation I have ever heard."

At which point Leonard Martin said: "The only problem is, he's trying to be a wolf!" Which the class thinks is the funniest thing they've ever heard. They laugh and they laugh and they laugh and then they all, and I mean every last one of them, get down on the floor in the squat position and start making rooster noises. The next day I find a drawing of a rooster on my locker, someone called my house later in the week asking for Rooster, I'd walk down the hall and hear rooster noises behind me...and years later we have a 28-year-old man from Ohio who answers to the name "Rooster."

A bit of background on my parents. They aren't, let's say, very motivated people. My dad has worked in the same automotive plant since he was twenty. You know on your rearview mirror there's that warning "Objects in mirror are closer than they appear?" That's what my dad does. He's paints that sentence on rearview mirrors. Five days a week. Forty-nine weeks a year. For thirty-four years straight.

He takes the family to the same hotel in Florida every spring for one week, and we go to the same campground in July for one week, every year. Thanksgiving at one grandparents' house, Christmas at the others, switch the next year.

Let me tell you a story that sums up my father: when I was fourteen, he was in a car accident. This was the most exciting thing that had ever happened in our family. Apparently he was backing out of his parking spot at the hardware store and there was a delivery truck full of lumber in the aisle and he backed right into it. You know why? Because the object in the rearview mirror ACTUALLY WAS CLOSER THAN IT APPEARED. You can't make up this stuff.

So I grew up restless but without ambition—because what would I have done with it? I wanted to leave one day and never come back and show all of them that I could do something more with my life than paint the same thing on the same thing in the same place every single same day.

Which is where Carl Pinberg comes in. He and I were in algebra together our sophomore year and then ended up in geography together our senior year, where we'd sit in the back and pass drawings of our classmates back and forth. One Monday Carl came in and said that his uncle was staying with them for the weekend and had been showing him pictures of the condos he was building in Costa Rica. Only Carl said it with an accent, Cossstahhh Reeeeecah.

It sounded so exotic and about as far away from Ohio as you could get. When I asked him where Costa Rica is, he said, "If I had a map I could show you." I said, "Yeah, I wish you did," only to realize he was messing with me—we were in geography class and the walls were covered with world maps. So he shows me on the wall this country in the middle of Latin America with oceans on both sides.

And then he delivers the line that kept me awake at night for the next eight months: "You can surf there."

If you could have picked the one thing in the world that seems the farthest away from where I sat at that exact moment in my life, it would be surfing. Something other people do in this far off place.

Carl told me his uncle was building condos in beach towns there and he thought he could find a job for Carl on a construction site and maybe even one for a friend the summer after they graduated from high school.

And then Carl looks at me and says, "So what do you say? Are you in?"

You have to understand, there was no plan for me. My dad got his factory job after high school and my mom worked in an appliance store until they were married and then they had kids and settled into the groove—also known as a rut— that they're still in.

I was never taught to dream or go after anything. Life just was what it was. But in that geography class something was planted inside of me. The infinitesimally small seed of hope that there might be a life for me beyond this small town in eastern Ohio.

So Carl and I planned and plotted. We'd drive over an hour to a big mall bookstore near Cleveland that carried Surfer magazine. We started using words like "gnarly" and "stoked." I actually got graded down on an essay on Pride and Prejudice in English class because I described how this one dude was really "stoked" to meet this girl, and my teacher thought it was something dark and sexual. When I was confronted by the teacher in front of my parents about my "explicit language," I explained that it was a surfing term. My mom tilted her head and asked all super concerned, "Donnie, where did you learn to talk like that?"

Carl and I wrote letters to his uncle. We did pull-ups in my basement. We rented Spanish language how-to CD's from the library. We ate a lot of bananas and mangos and pineapples. We told people that the day after graduation we were moving to Latin America to surf and live the dream. We actually used that phrase "Live the Dream." And meant it.

On graduation day, you know those square hats? We took tape and wrote "LTD" on the top of our hats. Of course, my dad and other parents saw the LTD on our hats and assumed it was a reference to the car once made by Ford, which was not made in his factory, and therefore a blow to the family pride. When I explained it stood for "Living the Dream," he looked at me skeptically and said "Like when you're sleeping…?"

Of course, this was nothing compared to telling my parents that after graduation I was moving to Costa Rica with Carl Pinberg to work construction and surf and, well, live the dream.

After that long, awkward pause where they sat there digesting my plans, my dad finally said, "But saltwater makes your eyes sting."

Yep, that's what he said.

But they didn't try to stop me. I had saved up all senior year, and Carl and I had learned everything we could about where we were going. So we left.

I have a picture Carl took of me when we first landed and were waiting for Carl's uncle to pick us up at the airport. I'm squinting from the sunlight and look like I'm in pain. The sun was so bright and intense. And Carl's uncle never came because he forgot which day it was we were coming. So we hitchhiked from the airport to this little town where we were going to stay. Well, it's not really a town; it's more like a remote beach with little cabanas you can rent nearby.

Playa Avellenas is what it's called: Avellenas Beach. And it was everything I had been picturing for a year: White sand and people drinking smoothies under palm trees as they stared into the horizon where blue skies met turquoise waters. We unloaded our bags at the shack we were renting and then we immediately went down to the water where I got the most vicious sunburn I'd ever had. But I soldiered on. There were surfers in the water, lots of them, mostly beginners, taking lessons. When I suggested we rent boards and start surfing right away, Carl protested. "We have a chance to do this right, D, to start our surfing careers in epic form. Why should we paddle out among all these kooks?" For emphasis, Carl pointed to surfers who were riding giant foam boards, teetering and standing up on wimpy little two-foot waves and said, "Can you do that?"

I thought for a minute. "Sure. I've done my pull-ups."

"Of course you can. Do you think Kelly Slater or Laird Hamilton came to Costa Rica the first time and surfed those tiny little wimpy waves with beginners?"
"No."

"Exactly. That's my point. We should do it right or not do it. We both know real surfers wouldn't be caught dead paddling out there with those newbies. They would go to—"

"Witch's Rock."

And so without ever having ridden a board, I paddled out at Witch's Rock. I'd seen Witches Rock in a movie. It looked so easy to catch a wave there. But then we went and paddled out and I learned what it's really like. I'd get a little bit out and then a wave would come and it would look so small and harmless, but it would push me back toward shore. And I'd be paddling as hard as I could trying to get out but going back in toward shore— it was exhausting. It took me an hour to get a hundred yards out from shore. And the sun—I had never experienced such relentless heat. Hotter than hell. By the time I was far enough out to actually catch a wave, I was starting to feel nauseous.

Who gets seasick sitting on a surfboard?

Not real surfers, that's who. So I'm hot and sweaty and wet and I have that gnawing feeling like I'm going to vomit— which I did. So then I'm paddling away from my own throw-up, which is floating there on the surface of the water, taunting me, egging me on, reminding me that I am a long way from home.

I calm myself down, I psych myself up, and I resolve to catch the next wave. I'm convinced that as soon as I catch my first wave I'll be fine. Then a set comes through, and I paddle as hard as I can into it. I feel the most exhilarating rush as this massive sound comes up behind me, my board pitches forward, I grab the rails and stand up...assuming that I'll find myself riding the wave. I'll be surfing.

Only it doesn't happen.

I'm staring not at the shore, or the shoulder of the wave, but at the water, which means that this wave is much larger than it first looked. It's so large that it has thrown me out the front, and I am without my board, flying through the air like I've just jumped off a diving board. I hit the water hard. Like knock-your-breath-out-of-you hard. Just as I ask myself, "Where is my board?" it hits me in the back of the head. Now I'm dizzy.

The wave then crashes on top of me, pushing me under the water, where I slam into sharp rocks just below the surface. The same rocks, it turns out, that my leash gets caught on, the strap that connects my foot to the board, holding me under the water.

In surfing terms, this is called the "spin cycle." It's when you get caught up in a wave that is so strong it causes you to tumble end over end so that you lose your sense of up and down.

Which was the least of my problems. Did I mention that I'd forgotten to hold my breath as I went under?

I managed to get the leash free and find my bearings enough to swim to shore, where I crawled up on the beach and sat there with my head between my knees. It was so embarrassing. I realize now that it wasn't as much humiliation as it was fear. I was terrified. I thought I was going to drown. And so I sat there on the beach at Witch's Rock in the Guanacaste region of Costa Rica, trying to get my chest to stop heaving because I almost got myself killed the first time I ever went surfing. It was the loneliest moment of my entire life. And where was Carl? He showed up two hours later. He had paddled too far out and gotten caught in the current that took him two miles down the beach where he had to be rescued by some fisherman who took him back to the river mouth where he met some girls from Portugal who invited him to eat lunch with them on the beach. Carl came back to tell me that he'd really hit it off with one of the girls, and he was going back to the resort where she was staying to have dinner with her family.

Me: "Do you even know any Portuguese?"
Carl: "I know a little Portuguese and she knows a little American."
Me: "I can't believe you just said that."
Carl: "Seriously, D, we both know that love is the only language anyone needs to speak."

I never saw him again.

I went back to our cabana that night and lay on the bed throbbing with pain from the sunburn and the places where the coral cut my skin and gashed my forehead...but do you know the worst part, the part that told me that I was never going to make it there?

My eyes stung. All night. By the morning I could barely see they were so swollen. And do you know what made them sting?

The salt water.

What hurt more than my eyes was my ego—which could not even begin to face the fact that maybe my dad was in some small way...right. The possibility of that being true made me ache all over.

The next morning I went to the construction office to get my assignment and no one was there. I asked around for Carl's uncle only to find out that he wasn't "involved in the project anymore."

Could it get any worse?

I still had some money left so for the next two weeks I drank cheap red wine in the shade of a palm tree and ate bananas and stared out at the ocean and cursed my family and my pale skin and my town and my heritage and the state of Ohio and the fact that I was going to have to go home and move back into my bedroom in my parents' basement and find a shitty job and drive the same shitty car and end up just like everybody else in my shitty family in my shitty town in my shitty life.

I vaguely remember the next three years. They barely exist to me. I lived with my parents and I delivered pizzas and I painted houses and I tried to do this discount long distance phone pyramid "business opportunity" and I worked at a car wash and I went to a training seminar to become an insurance agent but then left the moment they said we would build our portfolio from cold-calling.

Hell is cold-calling people asking them how much money their loved ones would get if they unexpectedly died later that day.

Eventually I got a job at a hotel, sweeping the floor of the lobby and assisting the front desk and generally doing the things no one else wanted to do. It was a medium-sized hotel with several conference rooms and a pool and a breakfast buffet and free cable and a glass elevator with a lovely view of the koi pond in the middle of the lobby. I had been there four or five months and it was another boring day in my boring life as I did my rounds of the conference rooms, making sure everybody had what they needed when I noticed that whatever was happening in 403B, it was really quiet in there.

This is a room that seated 350, so for it to be full and quiet struck me as odd. I slipped in the back and there on the stage was this guy—some sort of motivational speaker, and as my eyes adjusted to the darkness of the room and the glare of the spotlights on the stage he yelled, "It's time for you to pick yourself up by your—" Then he paused and the crowd yelled, "BOOTSTRAPS!" It was like a bomb going off. They exploded. People standing and clapping, music came on over the speakers, whistling and shouting and cheering, the release was unreal. I had never seen anything like it. And there he stood, on the stage, like a quarterback who'd just won the Super Bowl. It was amazing. I had no idea what this was, or who he was, but it was overwhelming.

I went out in the hall, found the sign, and read "2 p.m. Yves Green." Yves? Who has a name like that? How do you even pronounce it?

Then people came pouring out of the room, and they were amped. Many of them headed straight for a table that had books on it and made a line. The energy in that hall was just like the energy in the conference room. Like they'd all plugged into the same socket or they'd been drinking the same juice. I changed an ashtray, I straightened a sign, I refilled some water pitchers, I acted very busy so I could hang around.

And then he appeared. He sat down at the table, he looked people in the eyes, he asked their names, he signed their books. I was star struck by someone I'd never heard of before ten minutes prior.

Then a tall woman said, "I just bought the last book!"

Which prompted the person in line behind her to say, "What? Are you serious?" Only they said it like someone had just announced that the world was ending in five minutes. Panic.

"Excuse me, do you work for the hotel?" He was talking to me. I nodded. "Could you be a hero and go to my car and get the box of books out of the trunk?"

And without waiting for my response, he tossed me his keys. "Blue station wagon, closest spot to the back door."

So I did. Only I ran. My heart was beating. I was on a mission. THESE PEOPLE NEEDED THESE BOOKS, and I had the keys to get into his car to get the books...of course I had no idea what he was about or what his book was about. It could have been 101 Favorite Nazi Recipes or How to Make Smart Bombs out of Dish Detergent, Jumper Cables, and Dead Cats, but that was beside the point.

I was needed. For something that mattered.

So I got the books, I unpacked the box, I helped distribute the books and make sure he signed them. I got him water. In the course of an hour, I was sucked into the vortex that is the world of Yves Green—and I loved it. He stayed until he'd talked to every last person who wanted to talk and then I helped him pack up his sign and the few books that were left and I carried them to the car with him and helped him load up.

It was cold that night. I remember that part. I just stood there next to his car as he got in and closed the door. I didn't want him to go. I was a loser. He was a winner. That much was very clear to me. And for a brief moment, I was let into the winner's circle. And I didn't want to leave. He rolled down his window, "I'll be back tomorrow—could you give me a hand again?"

"Yes." And he drove away.

The next morning I wasn't working, but I put on my hotel uniform and went back, and this time I heard the whole talk and it was about ambition and dreams and goals and picking yourself up by your bootstraps. He told us where the "bootstraps" phrase came from and he gave all of these historical examples from the founding of America about how people settled in different areas and against all odds built towns and railroads and schools...I don't think I breathed for most of it. It was unlike anything I had ever experienced. And the other people listening were clearly having the same experience, which made it even more powerful.

I wasn't alone. For the first time, I wasn't alone.

After his talk I helped him sell books and I got water, and because I knew the hotel staff, I got his room rental extended for another hour for free, and I organized which people wanted which books signed and who wanted a picture with him. It felt so natural to be working for this man.

We ended up back at his car, loading up, standing there in the cold, when he offered me the job. He said he was taking his game to "a whole new level," which sounded totally awesome to me at the time, and he was going to need a "dedicated team" who all knew their roles and could "work together as one." He said he saw something in me, a fire, a hunger, a desire, and he also said he saw organizational skill—an "extraordinary attention to detail" is how he put it.

Me? I didn't know what he was talking about. But if it was getting me a job, and maybe a new life, I was in. We met the next day and he explained that there would be lots of traveling, that he was starting to get opportunities outside of Ohio and that would mean we'd be all over the country, and I would need to be able to go anywhere at anytime. "Still interested?" he asked me.

Can you imagine what that was like for me? I was going to need to be available to go all over the country. This was too good to be true. When our meeting was over, and I'd officially accepted the position of "Director of Logistics" for Yves Green, up-and-coming motivational speaker, I went out to my car and sat there and sobbed. Not out of fear, or terror, or the despair that I didn't belong, but sobs of joy because I did belong. (By the way, I don't cry a lot-those are the only two times I can remember actually crying. If you don't count the 73 times I tear up during that ridiculous story about the girl in Peru.)

I didn't tell my parents. I'd learned my lesson. They were used to me switching jobs a lot so when I stopped wearing the hotel uniform, they didn't say anything, I waited for the day when we travelled by plane for the first time and then told them casually at breakfast, "Oh yeah—" I paused.

"I won't be around the next few nights."

My mother: "Well, where will you be staying?"
Me: "Oh...I need to be in New York for work..." And I just let it linger there. This was a new day.
I had a life. I was going to milk this moment for all its worth.

My dad: "New York, Ohio?"
My mom: "There's a town in Ohio named New York? I didn't know that, well, that's certainly confusing..."
Me: "No, New York. The New York. NYC."

And for the next seven years, which are also the past seven years, I have been to New York often (13 times) as well as every major city in this fine land of ours. I have been on trains and buses and planes and vans and taxis, and I have stayed in every form of hotel and motel, and I have eaten in every kind of restaurant and food stand and cocina and kiosk and market there is. And I have watched thousands and thousands of people experience Yves Green, and I have watched them buy his books and take his picture and I have organized every kind of event a motivational speaker does.

Want sushi in Cleveland? Looking for a workout facility that's open on New Year's Eve in Rhode Island? Need an SUV that fits seven with snow chains to go up a mountain in Idaho the day after Christmas when all of those cars have already been rented?

That's me. I can find it, rent it, book it, reserve it, fix it, arrange it, pull it off, make it appear, create it out of thin air, all without anybody actually knowing just what a pain it was to make it happen. And through it all, I have always made sure that he has his water. Like right now, I've got him his water and I'm just giving it to him and I'm realizing that the signing line may even be longer than it was when I left, and he's talking to someone who has just asked him,

"So you've been to Europe?"
Yves: "Yes, I spoke there last year."
"That's great. Do you know Sven?"
Yves: "I may—do you know where I may have met him?"
"Well, he lives in Europe. And I figured since you've been there..."

Right. This person knows someone who lives in Europe and Yves has been to Europe, so does Yves know this person? It's

all I can do not to look at him and say, "You remember—Sven.
About medium height, brownish hair, loves soccer?" But I've
learned it's really better when I keep such thoughts to myself.

Friend of Sven has gotten his book signed and next were
several married couples and a group from a local business and
two super fans with bootstraps tattoos ("This way we'll never
forget!") and then a group of college age girls are standing
there staring at Yves when one of them says, "I totally relate to
your stories" and they all nod and keep staring.

You do? Seriously, you do?
You relate to his stories?
Your whole village was sick and about to die?
You have a donkey?
You live in a village in Peru?
You went up over the mountain and got the medicine?
Is there one detail in even one of his stories that has even one
thing to do with your life?

They leave and now we have a short man who is trying to
speak to Yves, but his English is not so good. Yves is stooped
over and the man is doing all he can to communicate, and I
notice Claudia has come over. Whatever the man wants to say,
he's giving it everything he has:

"Millones cojones..."

Yves lights up. "Yes, that's right, millones cajones!"
The man: "No, lo siento, sorry, not millones cajones."
Yves: "I'm sorry, I didn't get that last part..."

Yves is too polite. I would have said to the man by now: "Three words: Learn the language."
But the man trudges on:

"I do not think you think you say right words."
Yves: "Oh yes, you said it right—millones cajones."
The man: "No, no, what you say is 'millones cojones' that is how it says—"
Yves: "I'm sorry, I'm not understanding what you mean."

It's getting a bit tense. Claudia is leaning in, I've stepped forward, Yves is working really hard here to stay calm and kind, but the man won't give up. "You're not say it right. You need to say 'millones de dolares cojones' because I hear millones cajones."

Whatever his point, I'm sensing it's important. Yves doesn't, because he says, "Oh, you'd like to buy a Millones Cajones shirt, or was it a book? And you don't have American dollars? No problem, you know what? I'm going to give you the book and the shirt, how's that? For free—and should we have our picture taken together as well?"

Okay, I don't know any Spanish, but I am pretty sure this man isn't asking for free stuff.

What's this? Claudia just found someone in the line who speaks Spanish. Told you she was good. The man says something to the interpreter who then says to Yves: "What he's saying is that 'millones cajones' translates literally 'millions drawers,' and he doesn't think you mean that the girl in the story has millions of drawers. He says what you're trying to say is 'millones de dolares cojones,' which is how a person would say 'million dollar balls." Yves gives him a blank look.

Interpreter: "He says your title is a mistranslation. It doesn't mean what you think it means. So everybody who knows Spanish sees your book or hears your talk and it doesn't make any sense to them." The interpreter then turns to Yves and says, "He would like to know, do you know any Spanish?" Yves, without missing a beat, says,"Why yes, I now know four words: millones de dolares cajones!"

And the interpreter laughs and Yves laughs and Claudia laughs as the man turns and walks away. I suddenly realize we need to get Yves out of there really fast and Claudia agrees because she says to the few people still remaining, "We're sorry, but Yves is late to his next engagement." And we're off...down the hall through the dressing rooms, grab our things, then out the side door into a waiting van.

Y

I feel like I've been kicked in the stomach. Is the title of the book wrong? Does the title Millones Cajones make no sense? Just the image of millions of cojones—it's disturbing. Does everybody who speaks Spanish sit there when I'm talking and think, "What an idiot—he means to say 'million dollar cojones' but instead he's saying 'millions testicles'"?

And now Rooster is saying something…

R

Yves seems dazed. Like someone kicked him in the stomach.

Me: "You okay?"
Yves: "It's that last man, the one speaking Spanish—"
Me: "Yeah, that was a little awkward."
Yves: "But what he said—what do you think?"
Claudia: "I think Jose needs to work on his English."
Yves: "But his point was that my Spanish needed work…"
Me: "Well, it does."
Yves: "But I don't pretend to speak Spanish."
Me: "You titled your book in Spanish and your talk centers around a Spanish phrase and you tell a story about a Peruvian girl who speaks Spanish—that gives people a certain impression."

Noll (whom Claudia has just brought up to speed): "Let me get this straight. A man waited in that signing line for a half hour to tell you that 'millones cajones' means-

Claudia (Holding up her phone): "Actually it says here that cajones means drawers in Spanish, and cojones means guts or balls or gonads or testicles…"

Noll: "Thank you, babe. So you wanted to say 'million dollar balls' but for people who know Spanish it sounds like you're saying 'millions of testicles'?" And we're just now finding out about this?

Pause.

Yves: "Well…yes."

Noll: "Did you check with anyone who actually speaks Spanish before you sent the book to your publisher?"

Yves: "No."

Noll: "Did anyone at the publisher check with someone who actually speaks Spanish to see if the title made any sense?"

Yves: "I have no idea."

Me: "Which means no."

Noll: "Now that's funny—"

Yves: "Unless it's your name on the book."

Me: "And the shirts and the posters and for a while the beach chair—"

Yves: "Thank you, Rooster, for the reminder."

Noll: "I still think that beach chair was an awesome idea. How many other motivational speakers do you know who have their own beach chairs? I still have some of them in my garage…"

N

Sometimes I think Rooster is getting too cynical. Yves and I loved that beach chair idea. I know they didn't sell that well, but it was a statement. Sometimes it's about making a statement.

Y

Enough dwelling on that. Time to shift gears. It's important that I can leave things behind and focus on the next thing. Dinner with Lou, my agent. He's an engine. Never stops pushing. Always looking out for me. Always thinking ahead.
He happened to be here in Charlotte for the evening and whenever we can, we sit down for a meal. Lou knows every great restaurant in every city in the world. Tonight he's picked some new Asian fusion place but I don't notice much about it because I'm tired, I'm hungry, I'm bothered, I'm haunted by that man, by that conversation. I swear that took a year off my life, just trying to understand what he was saying and being polite and kind when I wanted to yell, "Learn the language!"

The sad part is that I didn't know whether to yell it at him... or myself.

R

Lou Snell. Yves calls him an engine, and that's the best way I can think of to describe him. Loves to eat, always picks the

restaurant, never fails to find us an amazing meal. I can find
anything, anywhere, but Lou? Lou Snell can smell anything
anywhere. We know if we're going to be in the same town that
we'll get a text, something like "Palms on 5th at 6" and we go.
And it's always good. So here we are at a new place called
Chopstix and it's new and funky and there he is in the back at
a big round table...

L

What a team. Every time I see them together I am reminded
how strange the world is. Yves and then Noll, who I swear was
a secret agent of some sort, probably still is. Whenever I ask
him about his past, anything between his time in the Marines
and when he went to work for Yves, he's really vague. He'll say
he was traveling or doing sales work or he was "overseas."
That's my favorite—"overseas"—could he be any more
mysterious? And then there's Claudia, who I adore. Orange
tiger stripes in hair tonight, very nice. And then Rooster, and
yes...he's carrying his clipboard. He's an odd one...

R

Lou thinks I'm weird. My sense of humor, he never seems to
get it. Like the fact that one of his clients is a singer named
Yolanda Yolanda. For real. She does this techno dance sort of

thing with bagpipes. I always ask him, "How's Yolanda Yolanda doing doing?"

Somewhere in the course of the meal—I had the shrimp lo mein—this exchange takes place:

Yves: "Lou, I've been thinking. Maybe it's time we should reposition me in the market. I've been reading this book on Blue Ocean—"
Lou: "Dr. Kim?"
Yves: "Who?"
Lou: "Dr. Kim, that's who wrote the book, along with Renee Mauborgne. We had a meal once, Dr. Kim and I, in Bordeaux, I believe I had the mahi mahi with an absolutely extraordinary chardonnay."
Yves: "So I've been thinking: people see me as what?"
Lou: "What?"
Yves: "That's my question: how do people see me?"
Lou: "How? Or what?"
Me: "They see you as a motivational speaker because that's what you are."
Yves: "Thank you, Rooster. But could we change that? Is there some other way to describe what I do that would set me apart?"
Lou: "And move you from the Red Ocean to the Blue Ocean?"
Yves: "Exactly!"
Noll: "You lost me…"

Claudia: "Me as well."

Yves: "Sorry. Here's the idea: Most businesses compete in a Red Ocean market. They're going against each other and so they constantly have to cut their price while at the same time raising their quality, and they duke it out with other similar products or services, each of them vying for the same slice of the same pie, fighting over the same customers."

Noll: "like Coke and Pepsi, Dominoes and Little Caesars, Avis and Hertz—"

Yves: "Yes. But then there are companies who make something or offer something that is so unique and different, they aren't really competing with anybody...they don't compete within the same slice of the pie, they create a whole new pie, they move—"

Noll: "From a Red Ocean to a Blue Ocean."

Yves: "Exactly."

Lou: "In the book, they give the example of Cirque du Soleil. Everybody said the circus industry was dead, that there wasn't any more money to be made, etc. What the Cirque people did is get rid of the animals and the three rings and the traditional music and even the high paid performers and created something totally new by fusing theatre and ballet and gymnastics and modern music—and then they raised tickets prices and they're making a killing."

Lou loves that phrase "making a killing"—it's his highest accolade. If he comes to hear Yves speak, he'll say afterwards,

"You killed them" or "Man, did he kill it or what?" Noll has totally checked out. He's fascinating like that. If we leave the pragmatic and black and white, he doesn't come with us. So with a discussion like this, if it's not about the next thing we're doing or a problem that needs to be solved right now, he just isn't interested.

Yves: "So what would a Blue Ocean look like for me? I think I have an answer. I think I should stop referring to myself as a motivational speaker."
Claudia: "So what would you be?"
Yves: "An aspirational speaker."
Me: "And you could spell it with two s's!"

Noll thinks that's hilarious, but Lou looks at me like I should crawl under the table.

Yves: "No, seriously. What if I repositioned myself as an aspirational speaker? I could do a whole campaign and promotional thing. I could explain that I'm not about motivating, which is what pushes people from behind, I'm about aspiring, what pulls people into the future. "It isn't about what's driving you, it's about what's inspiring you…"
Me: "Is that even a valid distinction? I don't get it."
Lou: "It doesn't matter if it makes any sense to you—it matters if people remember it."

Noll: "And if they'll buy things with 'aspirational' written on them."

Lou: "So every time someone anywhere says 'motivational speaker' we'll correct them with 'aspirational speaker'"?

Yves: "Yes."

Lou: And when I'm booking you, and I'm on the phone with a promoter or another agent or a corporate representative, I would talk about the aspirational speaker I represent, as in "Oh no, you're going to have to pay him way more, he's an aspirational speaker..."

Yves: "Exactly."

Claudia: "I like it."

Are we really having this conversation? Are we actually considering this idea? Am I losing it? Are they losing it? If somebody asked me what I do for a living, would I say from now on: "I work for an aspirational speaker"? How embarrassing.

Yves: "Rooster, what do you think?"

Me: "I'm in if we spell it with two s's."

And so we eat and talk and plan and Lou asks about the EXPLODE weekend, and we give him updates and we talk about what's going on between now and then and he and Yves talk about some publishing issues that I'm not a part of and then we say good-bye to Lou Snell, soon to be agent of the world's first ever aspirational speaker, and we're off to a club around the corner to meet with some representatives from a teachers' association who are bringing Yves in to speak at their annual convention in four months. They're the typical kinds of people who organize events: perky and upbeat, and they want Yves to inspire and challenge and entertain and not say anything offensive and I've heard this a thousand times. Everybody wants the same thing. CEO's and Firefighters and Pilots and Athletes and Managers and people with Greenhouses in cold climates (G.I.C.C.—they have a conference each year) and senior citizens groups and soft drink companies.

Everybody wants to be inspired and challenged and entertained, and they don't want anybody to be offended... heard it, heard it, heard it. And Yves is totally engaged, taking notes, asking them questions about their organization and the teachers and what ages they teach and what their unique struggles are. He tells them what he's going to speak about and they love it. Here in leather chairs in the back of a club with a few drinks he's doing what he does in massive rooms with hundreds of people—winning them over. These folks leave totally assured their event is going to be a smash success. By now it's 9 and everybody is cooked. Exhausted. To the hotel we go, everybody to their rooms, until we meet in the hotel bar at 9:30 because Yves wants to get a start on the EXPLODE Applications.

Have I explained the EXPLODE weekend yet?

Y

I would give anything to go to sleep now. But if I call off our 9:30 that will send the wrong message, and I can't do that. It's moments like these, when every bone in my body wants to go to sleep, that the great ones keep going. And so, for the umpteenth time, I reach down and I keep going. Bag on the bed, splash face, brush teeth, change shoes, down to the bar.

C

I don't know how I got put in charge of the EXPLODE applications. There must be a hundred here and there are still two months to go. I think I'm in charge of it because it was my idea, or at least it was my idea to think about a better idea. And then Rooster jumped in about the money and Yves had the EXPLODE theme, which he said he'd been thinking about for a while, and so we did it. We put the word out, and here we are, here I am, with a stack of applications.

Y

I think EXPLODE was Claudia's idea. It was so against everything I believe in at first, I couldn't even begin to understand it. But then Rooster jumped in and I saw it. Their premise was basically this: I talk to all these people, but who is actually going to do the things I talk about? What percentage of people actually change? What percentage of people buy the book and cheer for the talk and get the t-shirt, but they don't actually do the hard work of becoming a better person? So am I wasting my time on people? That was the question I had a problem with. I've always said I'll talk to anybody, anytime, anywhere. That's how I've got this far. Their proposal was to do a one-time event, for a select group of people, only people I choose. People who have proven they take seriously what I say.

Interesting. And then Rooster suggested they could fill out applications, answering some essay questions to give us a chance to see what they're made of. And then Noll said we could charge three thousand dollars a person for three days. And they would cover their own expenses, which, if three hundred people came, would be a lot. Nine hundred thousand dollars, for three days of work. And no planes and no vans and no taxis. And then Claudia suggested we could do it at a resort, and I could have a suite with a personal chef who would make me whatever meals I wanted. Nice.

I remember asking, "You're telling me that people would pay three thousand dollars to hear me talk for three days?"
Noll: "They would pay five thousand if they could."

I'd had this idea to do something about explosions, how certain chemicals collide with other chemicals and certain substances are mixed with other substances and that's what makes explosions. It's the perfect metaphor because it's like that with hard work. It isn't just hard work that gets you ahead —it's smart hard work. It isn't just being in the right place at the right time, but it's knowing what to do when you're there. So our success is actually an explosion that is the result of the alchemy between several different elements: hard work and perseverance and attitude and being in the right place at the right time... And so I developed this whole explosions- themed event and it clicked. EXPLODE was born.

And when we put the word out, we got 48 applications back the next week. By the end of the month we had over 300.

I haven't seen any of them, but Claudia says they're very impressive, and so here we sit, in the bar of the hotel, at 9:30 on a Thursday night in Charlotte, about to see just what we've gotten ourselves into.

R
Claudia suggests we take the applications, divide the stack in four, and then we each read the one in front of us, then we all vote on whether that applicant should be accepted, and so on.

So she goes first:

"This is Owen Fortem from Portland and he writes 'I have read every one of Yves Green's books and watched every video and read every article and seen him live every time he has come to Portland and I would consider it an honor to sit at his feet for a weekend.'

Me: "'Sit at your feet'?"
Yves: "Yes, it's a sign of respect, like the Eastern sages, whose disciples would sit at their feet and learn. I like this guy…"
Me: "Sounds creepy. Stalkerish."
Claudia: "Do you want me to continue?"
Yves: "Nope, he's in."

I go next:
"My name is Harry Montague and I totally dominate my Wednesday night softball league. I own a business I started in my garage three years ago. We clean people's fish tanks. I've taken all the lessons I've learned from Mr. Green and applied them to our business and it's made all the difference. We are now the number one fishtank-cleaning business in the tri-cities area."

Harry gets a thumbs up.
And on it goes, we read these for an hour until we're all barely staying awake. Once again, this should be terribly exciting and inspiring—this is the biggest, riskiest thing we've ever done,

renting a resort and charging people this kind of money and taking applications. This should be an incredibly rewarding experience for seven years of backbreaking hard work, but I'm just not feeling it. To bed we go. Breakfast at 7.

Y

'Tell me about today, Rooster.'

R

I put down my fork. I grab my clipboard. 'This morning is Shawanee Elementary School—it's their 'Don't be a Bully' week, and you're wrapping up three days of guest speakers. And then we do applications for an hour and then you're speaking at the Minor League Baseball Experience Managers Annual Conference, and then—"

Yves: "The what?"
Me: "It's the association of people who work for minor league baseball teams who are in charge of all those giveaways and contests during the game."
Yves: "They have an association?"
Me: "They do, and you're speaking to them, in four hours."
Yves: "What am I speaking to them about?"

Me: "I don't know, six months ago when you said yes, you said you'd think of something. I believe your exact words were, 'I have six months, I'll think of something...'"

Noll: "I went to this minor league baseball game last year, and it was British humor night. They had this guy dressed up from Monty Python, with that chain mail hat-hood thing and tall leather boots, and behind him was a guy banging two coconuts together making the sound of horses' hooves like in the movie. They galloped around the stadium for the whole night, and it was hot—really hot, and the guy never took off his metal chain mail hood. He was dripping with sweat, and I thought he was going to pass out. That's the kind of dedication I like to see."

Rooster: "Did anybody in the crowd get it?"

Noll: "I doubt it. British humor is a bit of an acquired taste. And minor league baseball crowds don't seem like the folks who would most appreciate it."

Yves: "So these people I'm talking to—"

Me: "In four hours—"

Yves: "—in four hours. These people are the ones in charge of coming up with ideas like British humor night?"

Me: "Yep. And most of these teams play at least fifty home games in a season, usually more, so they have to come up with a ton of new ideas."

There is a silence around the table for the next few minutes.
We're eating our breakfast realizing that Yves has no idea what
he's getting into.

Me: "And then in the afternoon you have an interview with a
local radio station for a show called "What's Happening Now!"
and then we've got tickets to hear Chuck Flannel.

Yves: "That's tonight?"
Claudia: "Yes, and we're going to go backstage and meet him
afterwards."
Yves: "We are?"
Claudia: "Yes, you said two months ago that the best thing you
can do to the competition is make friends with them."

Y

After breakfast I have a ritual. I go back to my room, I go over
the talks I'm giving that day, and then I call Khloe, my wife. I
am weary. And it's only morning. Today I take the elevator. I
always take the stairs—why would you not want the extra
workout? Elevators are for those who give up on the little
things. And the little things add up, don't they?

But today I am in the elevator on my way up before I even
realize what I've done.
Did the others see me get on?

Noll: "Did you see that?"

Claudia: "What?"

Noll: "Yves—he took the elevator!"

Rooster: "No way, seriously? That would be a first..."

Y

Me: "Hey, babe."

Khloe: "Morning."

Me: "What's new?"

Khloe: "I think our little Charis has a special friend who's a boy."

Me: "No way."

Khloe: "He called here yesterday. He was so nervous. I gave him a hard time, just to see how he handled it."

Me: "What's his name?"

Khloe: "Greg."

Me: "Greg?"

Khloe: "Greg Dodge. And he fancies our girl."

Me: "This is new territory."

Khloe: "Yes it is, and you should have seen her face when I handed her the phone and told her it was a boy. She was so embarrassed. She blushed. I can't imagine what she'd done if you were here. She would have been mortified."

Me: "Then I would have blushed."

Khloe: "And how about you?"

Me: "Fine. The usual. I killed it yesterday. And then we started in on the EXPLODE applications, you'd love reading them. Great people coming. And you?"

Khloe: "Big one today, I'm meeting with vendors from the Boardwalk in Atlantic City. They're coming here. I was warned they're classic old school New Jersey Tough-guy business types—I can't wait to break them in half."

Me: "You really enjoy that part, don't you?"

Khloe: "Love it."

And she does. She really loves the negotiating part. Sometimes I wonder if my job is to find where people are strong, and her job is finding out where they're weak. It started one Fourth of July six years ago. We were having a party and trying to figure out what drinks to serve, and she decided to mix lemons, limes, water, and Stevia, that natural herbal sweetener. It was great. The best lemony-limey sort of drink I'd ever had. We stood there in the kitchen trying to figure out why it was so good. We realized that I had left half an orange in the blender that had been mixed in with lemon and lime. Kind of like a secret ingredient. When I asked her what she called her concoction, she immediately said: "Big Girl Lemonade." And then I added some tequila to mine and asked her what she'd call that, and she said: "Bigger Girl Lemonade." At the party people could not stop asking her what it was called and every time she said Big Girl they laughed. It caught on. At one point I was walking through the kitchen, and Khloe was surrounded by women and one asked for the recipe and she said no. I couldn't believe it. She smiled and said it was top-secret and that if she told them how she made it, she'd have to kill them. My wife. She is a rare one.

So the next time I returned from a trip guess what she's wearing? A t-shirt that says "Big Girl Lemonade" in giant letters and then below it, "Strong Enough for a Woman, Weak Enough for a Man." She explained that she'd decided to start a business selling her brew. She'd gotten a tax ID number and ten of her friends agreed to be investors and a local produce broker committed to providing her all the lemons and limes and oranges she needed and just like that she became a mogul.

A lemonade mogul.

She trademarked the phrase the next week and soon she'd convinced a local distributor to let her pitch it to bars. It was a hit. What person in a bar wouldn't love saying "I'll have a Bigger Girl?"

To be honest, Big Girl is her life. That and our daughter Charis. So it doesn't surprise me to learn that she'll be in a room later today filled with tough businessmen who she will then pulverize with her presence. I went to one of her pitches once. It was to the operations officer of a university—she was trying to get Big Girl sold at their campus events. She began by slowly pouring him a glass and talking about how the earth is our friend and taking care of ourselves is the greatest gift we can pass on to the next generation, and then she launched into the history of Stevia and its compound makeup and how good it is for the body and how we need innovation and fresh thinking or we're going to lose our way and how Big Girl Lemonade is an example of the kind of forward thinking his university prides itself on, and then she ended by asking him,

"What else are you gonna do—serve Coke?" Of course she got the account.

R

Where is Yves? He's never late, and we're due at the school in twenty minutes.

Y

I'm sitting on the edge of the bed in a hotel room that feels very, very lonely. For years this has been my ritual and I have loved it: Breakfast with my team where we go over the day ahead, a call to Khloe, and then I hit the ground running. But here I sit on the edge of the bed in a hotel miles from any sort of home, and it seems like so much work just to get to the shower. And then yesterday I had that moment in the hallway.

R

I ask our driver to push it, slip him a twenty, and we're there. Honestly, I find these school gigs a bit disturbing. Yves does his shtick about bullies and how some kids push and shove and it says more about them than you—the kids are with him the whole way. And then at the end, he asks them if he can give them a gift, and when they yell, "yes," he passes out these laminated lanyards that say "No Bully Here" on them. The kids love it. They put them on and wear them around like he just gave them gold on a string. Here's the part that I can't stomach: On the back in small letters is a website: "thrivingkids.com." And do you know what that is? A website Noll built that offers people a free download of a talk Yves does on raising "'Yes' kids in a 'No' world."

Actual discussion I keep having with Noll:
Me: "Isn't that kind of like what McDonalds does with Happy Meals?"
Noll: "How so?"
Me: "Well, the food at McDonalds is horrible for kids. It makes them fat while it clogs their arteries. So they offer kids a free toy that's worth maybe 5 cents that was probably made by another kid in some part of the world where they were paid 2 cents an hour and would be so grateful for a hot meal-the last thing they'd do is complain because it doesn't come with a toy —"

Yves jumps in: "So you're saying that my talk is like McDonald's food?"

Me: "I'm saying we give these kids these free lanyards about not being bullies, but you're doing it in the hope that when they show it to their parents later that day their parents will see the web address, download the talk, like it, and then buy your other talks and books and DVD's."

Noll: "Well said, Rooster, my good man. You have fully grasped our intent. It's called 'marketing.'"

Me: "But doesn't it seem just a bit questionable? You know, ethically, and all that?"

Noll: "Don't you want their parents to be inspired to live better lives? How is that a negative? What's ethically questionable about parents and kids living better lives?"

Me: "Money."

Yves: "Money?"

Me: "Yes, money. We—you—make money when people's lives get better."

N

Sometimes when Rooster gets on his rants I think to myself, "That boy needs some boot camp." He gets lost in the deep weeds on a regular basis, trying to reconcile profit and ethics and all sorts of things that he has no idea about. He needs to just stick to what he knows.

R

These discussions go nowhere. Yves and Noll know what they're doing, and it works and people buy it— literally buy it— which means I get a paycheck so I can buy a new Volkswagen like I just did, a GTI, the machine I have dreamed about for years, so why do I complain? Why do I keep raising these issues? Of course, I have only driven the car three times because we travel most of the year, going to things like the Minor League Baseball Experience Managers Annual Conference, which, judging by the chap who is walking towards us, should be quite an affair.

C

Have you ever talked to somebody on the phone and formed a picture of them in your mind and then met them and you were shocked? I'm the initial contact on almost everything Yves does, so by the time my contact actually shows up, I usually feel like I know whoever's running the event. Which is how I felt about Mort Sorner until this moment, meeting him.
I pictured tall and handsome and basebally, you know, hours in the sun, sports, the athletic type. But this man walking up to us, this can't be... yes, it is.

Him: "You must be Claudia?"
Me: "Yes, and you're Mort!" I smile like he's an old friend and looks exactly like what I thought he'd look like.

R

Claudia is so good. A man walks up to her wearing a massive t-shirt that says in big letters, "Minor League Baseball is the Sum Total of My Existence," only he's wearing the shirt OVER his dress shirt and tie and sport coat. And he's got on one of those Elmer Fudd hats, only he's jerry-rigged it with duct tape so it can hold two cans of beer. Got the picture? Claudia is unfazed. Obviously, this is who she expected because she seems so calm and gracious as she introduces us around.

Mort: "It is such an honor to have you all here. People are so excited—Yves Green is in the house!" He pumps his fists in the air and then, apparently because the awesomeness of the moment has overwhelmed him, Mort starts giving us high fives. Yves gets a high five, Noll gets a high five (by the way, he carries hand sanitizer in his pocket so when he has to shake a lot of hands, or in this case give high fives to strangers, he's prepared), Claudia gets a high five, and then what does Mort Sorner do when he gets to me? He chest bumps me.

Only this is not my high school reunion or the World Series—this is two guys who have just met in the lobby of a convention center at eleven thirty in the morning.

And one of them is wearing a hat with beer cans duct-taped to it.

Y
I have no idea what I'm going to say to these people. Five years ago I would have worked for days on my talk. I would have researched minor league baseball, giving myself a crash course in their world so I could speak directly to their challenges. I would have worked up an entire hour talk just for them—and I would have had it done months ahead of time, and I would have run it by Rooster and Claudia to see what they thought. And now, sitting here backstage, I am

confronted with the fact that in 17 minutes I am going to go
out there and talk to people I've never met about things I know
nothing about.

R

It occurs to me that Yves hasn't done his pre-talk ritual with us
where he gives us an idea of what he's going to say and we
give our feedback. He's just sitting there staring at the cheap
print on the wall.

Y

I used to love backstage rooms. The smells, the uncomfortable, abused furniture, the bad art. It's been home to me,
reassurance that I was living life in top gear, not sitting in some
office somewhere slaving for meaningless profit but doing
something, helping people, taking risks, out there in the world,
making my mark. Which I'm realizing right now makes me
sound a lot like a motivational speaker...those little backstage
carrots in the clear plastic container and the fake leather
matching couches and the metal folding chairs were symbols
of success to me. And now I'm sitting here noticing how
uncomfortable the couch is and how many thousand of these
little carrots I've eaten and how many hotel prints of
sunflowers I've stared at as I waited to go on stage and it isn't

fun anymore and it isn't challenging and it isn't worth it and it doesn't mean what it used to and I'm so tired…

R

I go to the back to watch, where I usually meet Claudia and Noll. Yves comes out to the lamest applause I've heard in a while—the room is dead. Some people are talking on cell phones, one man in front is typing on his laptop. Some are standing in the back, chatting. The just-after-lunch slot is killer—food is settling and they've already spent the morning being bombarded by whatever it is you bombard minor league baseball managers with…and Yves just stands there, staring at them. The room was quiet, but now it is silent. He just stands there and stares. The man on the cell phone is still talking, but now he's watching Yves intently. The couple in the back stops chatting.

And then Yves yells. Not specific words or a familiar sound, just a yell.

I look at Claudia, Claudia turns to Noll, Noll looks at me. He yells again. Louder than before.

It is quiet. No one is moving. The last bit of energy in the room has been sucked out.

More silence. He yells again.

Then he asks the crowd: Can anybody here yell louder than me?

Oh, this is hard to watch. It's like a car accident in slow motion.

He asks them again: "Can anybody here yell louder than I can?" Only this time it has a bit of edge to it, like it's a challenge, a dare, like he's ready to take on any challengers.

I consider for a moment pulling the fire alarm to end this agony, but as my eyes travel around the room looking for that little red metal square savior bolted to the wall, I hear from the front left corner: "I can."

Yves says: "Then come on up and show us what you got."

A woman stands up. She's probably in her late twenties, and she can't be more than a hundred pounds and she has long hair in a single pony tail and she's wearing a blue dress and she walks up, stands nervously next to Yves, and then she opens her mouth and yells "Cowabunga!" It's really, really loud, and a bit frightening. Far louder than Yves.

People begin to cheer. Somebody says, "Again!" She yells again. This time it's louder, way louder, scary louder. Like if this was your girlfriend and you were sitting in the audience, you'd be a little unnerved because she then rolls up her sleeves and yells even louder, putting her whole body into it. The crowd loves it.

Yves asks: "Can anybody top her?"

Instantly two different men are out of their seats and on the stage in moments. Yves nods to one of them and he opens his mouth, does this dramatic inhale in which he puffs up his chest, and then the weakest little whimper of a shout comes out. More like a squeak.

It's hilarious. Everybody is laughing. I look over at Claudia who is gasping for breath. This is truly funny. Yves nods to the other guy who does some sort of yodel on steroids in which he actually hits a note, like he's singing. Yves then nods to the first woman who does another one of her cowabunga shouts, but apparently because of the competition she has decided to take her game higher—she's in a whole new decibel range now. The crowd is now totally into it, and when Yves asks for a winner, the room is divided. He continues to egg them on, demanding they decide on a winner, which results in people shouting their favorite's name all the louder, bringing more and more energy to the room. He then calls for them to quiet down, and asks, "Is anybody wearing a tie?"

My chest-bumping buddy Mort Sorner raises his hand. Yves says, "Let me have it." As Mort makes his way to the stage, Yves announces with great flourish: "Ladies and gentlemen, Mort Sorner!" They cheer wildly. Mort Sorner smiles like a conquering king as he hands Yves his blue striped tie. Yves then asks the three shouter contestants to stand side by side. He ties the leg of one to the leg of another. He ask for another tie, gets it from a guy on the front row, and ties the other legs together. You know, like you do for a three-legged race when you were in third grade.

Yves then says to the crowd: "I bet these three can beat any of you three in a race around the outside of the room."

From the middle of the room: "No way, we could take them..."

Yves: "Let's see it!"

Up come these three men who proceed to tie their legs together using their white tube socks. Yves yells, "Go!" and six adults go careening around the banquet room of a hotel in the early afternoon. The crowd is cheering them on, yelling at them to go faster. People are moving chairs and tables out of the way to make a path. It is pandemonium. Then I notice another group of three making their way to the stage, taking off their ties... Contenders!

When the first team crosses the "finish line," Yves asks, "Who thinks they're faster?" Soon he's got three or four teams ready to go. People are sweating, rolling up their sleeves, re-tying their shoes. They are taking this seriously. I actually see one man stretching out before his race. Unbelievable.

After they wear themselves out on three-legged racing, Yves asks what they had for lunch, because many of the plates are still on the tables. When somebody mentions rolls, he asks if there are any left over. There are. He takes one, points to a trashcan in the far corner, and asks: "Who thinks I can make it?"

The crowd is divided.

He throws the roll, and it bounces off the front rim of the can, and lands on the floor. They groan. People who sat there staring at Yves with glazed expressions on their faces half an hour ago groan out loud because he just missed throwing a bread roll into a trash can fifty feet away. He then invites a woman up to try and she makes it. On the first try. Which then prompts almost every man in the room to rush up to the stage for their turn.

One guy has rolls stuffed into the pockets on the front of his shirt so he can get multiple tries. One man makes it on his fourth roll (he had some extras tucked in the front of his pants.

Gross.) and then does this sort of chicken dance victory strut that is hard to watch and yet they cheer him on. He is a hero. For five seconds.

Yves then organizes a game involving jumping over chairs and then the classic two-partner wheelbarrow race which, of course, they love. At the end of an hour of this, they're exhausted. One lady takes an inhaler out of her purse and passes it around! Yves then asks everybody to sit, but because of the mass pandemonium that has just ensued, there's no order to it. Some sit on chairs, others on their table, some are on the stage, some are on the floor, some have napkins wrapped like babushkas around their heads to absorb the sweat. Yves places a stool in their midst, sits on it, and asks, "What's the greatest stress of your job?"

At least ten of them immediately answer: "Budget."

He then asks them: "And how much did this past hour cost?"
Several murmur: "Nothing."
He leans forward, crosses his legs, and says: "Exactly. It didn't cost you anything. Bread rolls, ties, chairs—it was all here in the room. We just knew what to do with it. We were willing to be kids again. Isn't that why we go to the ballpark? It isn't about money and it isn't about corporations and it isn't about sponsorships—it's about families who want to come out to the ballpark and have a good time. Have any of you lost your

perspective? You got into this because you love baseball, because you have good memories of your parents taking you to games growing up that you wanted to be able to provide that same kind of experience for others. And then you get the job and you get a budget and you feel the pressure of having to come up with all these themes and programs and specials and you get swept up in the business and you lose the heart for the experience. Find that heart again, that heart that got you into this in the first place, and everything else will take care of itself."

Brilliant. I have been following Yves around the world, listening to him for years, and I have never seen him turn a crowd like this one. Where did he get the idea to do all of those crazy contests? How did he come up with that?

Absolutely amazing. And now they are hanging on his every word. He closes by thanking them, and then he stands up, pulls a roll out of his pocket he'd been saving the whole time, throws it across the room and into the trash can, and he walks out.

They give him a standing ovation. Mort Sornsen has tears in his eyes. Some of them are hugging each other. It's as if these people have just been to a religious revival. One of his best performances ever.

Y

I would love it if Rooster did not come back here. I would love
it if I could sit in this room alone for the next few hours. Or
days. I don't want to talk, I don't want to discuss, I don't want
to debrief. I just want to sit and not think about anything.

R

I cannot get backstage fast enough. I burst through the door.
Me: "Oh man oh man oh man!"
Yves says nothing, looks at me, and then looks back at the
pastel abstract framed on the wall.
Me: "Where did you come up with that? How did you know
that that yelling thing would work? And three-legged races?
When did you come up with all of that? You went for an hour
and a half! They loved it! They will be talking about that for
years. I gotta be honest, Yves, I thought that you'd forgotten to
prepare and that you were going to pull out some old talk
you've given before and just mail it in, go through the motions,
but instead you gave them the one thing they needed.
Amazing. Brilliant. And then the roll at the end—how did you
know to save just one and how did you know it would go in? If
you would have thrown that last one and it missed, it's not like
you could have just walked out like you did. But you tossed it
in like you knew it would go in, which made it perfect. It was
just perfect. Mort—you know, beer cans on hat minor league
baseball guy? Mort Sornsen was crying at the end. Crying.

Unbelievable. How did you know how to connect with that audience?

Y

I don't want to be having this conversation. I want Rooster to leave. I don't want to go out and shake hands and take pictures and sign books. I want to be done.

R

Seriously, Yves, you are going to sell a truck load of books today...you converted a lot of people today...they are going to spread the word about you...

Yves: "Do you want the truth?"
Rooster: "Yes, of course."
Yves: "No, you don't."

Y

Do I tell him I made it all up on the spot? Does he really want to know? Would it help him or confuse him to know I made it up on the spot? Should I tell him I had no idea what I was going to do or say until I got out on the stage and found myself standing there, all alone, with people who just didn't care? And once again, it was my job to turn the room around and make it an event and not just something to be endured. How many times do I do that? I enter a situation that is so lame, everybody just going through the motions, and take the room, I take the event, I take the people, and I put them on my back and I take them somewhere new. And every time I do it I give a little piece of myself away. Why is everybody so lame? Why are so many events so pathetic? Why are so many people so bad at this? Why do so many people need to be inspired? I'm tired of lifting people up. I'm tired of giving them a new perspective. I'm trying of breaking myself open and pouring myself out. The truth is, at that moment on that stage all I wanted to do was yell. I'm so exhausted. So I did. For once, I didn't think about the crowd and what they needed, I thought about what I needed. The rest just kind of happened. Is there even a remote chance Rooster could understand any of this?

"Rooster, here's what you have to understand: It didn't occur to me that the roll wouldn't go in. Nothing occurred to me. I just did it and came back here. Now could you please go tell Claudia that I'm not coming out to greet people and sign books? I'm going to stay back here."

R

Weird weird weird weird. Yves is losing it. I swear. That was the best thing he's ever done, absolute genius, and now he's cracking backstage.

C

"He what!? He's not coming out? What has gotten into that boy! I do believe that is the greatest thing any of us have ever seen him do and now he's announcing that he's not coming out? What am I going to tell Mort? They've made Yves his very own beer hat, and they want to have a presentation where they give it to him along with a pass that gets him and his family into every minor league ball park in the country for free —for the rest of his life. And he can't come out here? I will go back there and drag him out by his hair if I have to."

Y

Why is my phone ringing? Who would be calling me right now?
Yves: "Hello?"
Rooster: "Yves, I told Claudia what you said and she blew a fuse and said she's coming back to drag you out front if she has to...so heads up."

C

I find him staring at a painting on the wall, all alone, eating those little carrots. And he's unresponsive. I want an explanation, but he just mumbles something about how tired he is and how he just needs a little air. A little space. Noll will know what to do.

R

This is trouble. Noll has just invited the audience to come back
stage and have a party in Yves very own green room, because
"that's the kind of guy Yves Green is!" They follow him, at least
a hundred of them, down the back hall into the dressing room
area. They are packed in, and Yves comes to the door, and
they start cheering and taking pictures and Mort steps forward
and gives him the hat and the lifetime pass.

Y

And so I put on the double beer can hat, just like the sweater
yesterday, and just like the thousands of things I've tried on for
thousands of people for what feels like thousands of years...

R

They continue taking pictures and Yves signs a few books,
and then Noll announces that there's a sale on shirts
in the lobby and that's all they need to hear to leave.

Y

And finally they're gone. What is happening to me? I used to
love this. I used to love this. I used to love this. I used to love
this. I used to love this.

R

Me: "Claudia, help me understand."

Claudia: "You're asking questions above my pay grade, Rooster."

Y

My phone is ringing. Again.

Me: "Yes, Rooster?"

Noll: "It's not Rooster, Yves, it's Noll. I just covered for you and made you look great when the truth is you refused to come out. So the least you can do is explain yourself. What's going on?"

Me: "Noll, I'm tired. Not today sort of tired, or I just need some coffee tired, not I need a nap tired or I need a vacation tired, but bone tired, soul tired, existentially tired. Noll, I feel like I'm a thousand years old. I'm dead tired."

Noll: "Well, you may feel like you're a thousand years old, but you're selling a ton of books. Don't worry—I've got things under control."

Which is how Noll does things—the moment we start to get close to things like feelings and weakness and emotions, he reminds us all how he can handle it. Which strikes me as probably the first negative thought I've ever had about Noll. Am I turning on my own?

Get it together. Bootstraps. Gut it out. Time to deliver. Can't stay in here forever. Come on.

"Hey, Rooster—"

R

I'm being summoned. I go in the dressing room and see the palest looking Yves I've ever seen. "Yes?" "What's next?" "We're reading more applications and then Chuck—" "Let's scrap the applications, go to the hotel and crash, and then on to Chuck Flannel." "Fair enough. Sounds like a plan. Yves? Are you okay?" "Yep, great, just a little tired. Ate something weird earlier. I'll rally."

Now that is the Yves I know. He reaches down and he rallies and he makes a plan and he gets it done.

Y

So I'm sitting here in an auditorium next to Noll and Claudia and Rooster, and I'm watching people take their seats and I'm holding my ticket in my hand and I'm about to hear Chuck

Flannel for the first time and I'm suddenly aware that I have butterflies.

But I'm not speaking. I'm spectating tonight. It's a night off of sorts. I took them out for dinner and we're checking out the competition, but it's also my way of thanking them for all they do—you know, team spirit and all that...

R

It's strange that Yves considers going to see another motivational speaker a night off. Is this a sign that we're all losing it? We eat sleep and breathe all things motivational (aspirational) and then we get a night off and what do we do? We go to an auditorium that looks and smells and feels like the countless auditoriums we spend our days in, and we listen to someone else do what we do.

I just want to point this out for the record. It reminds me of that old guy in Shawshank Redemption who finally gets out of prison, but he's been in for so long that he can't deal with all of his new freedom and longs for the structure and boundaries of prison life so much he hangs himself...

So maybe not the best example.

But to be fair, I can't wait to hear this guy Chuck Flannel. He's new on the scene and the stories I've heard have to be overblown—no one is as good as they say he is. I keep tabs on who's new. Yves doesn't. But I do.

Y

Clean stage. Nice. No gimmicks or clutter. Nothing for sale in the lobby. This guy is clearly a rookie. There must be 400 people here. Good energy in the room. Have these people heard him before? Or are they first timers? I'd love to know that stat. Rooster will know. This is such a change of pace. I can't get over the fact that I'm not speaking tonight. I don't have any weight on me. I can experience this like everybody else must experience my events.

This should be normal, but I feel totally out of my element. Is that messed up? It's like I don't know how to function unless I'm performing. I actually thought about what I should wear tonight. I stood in front of the mirror in my hotel room and actually asked myself: "What do people wear to hear a motivational speaker?" Which led me to the question: "What are people wearing, Yves, when you look out from the stage pretty much every other night of the year?" Odd that I don't remember. Okay, here we go—house lights are going down.

R

They're playing classical music on the PA. Hmm… That can backfire on you if you're trying to get the energy up in the room. This guy is clearly a rookie. They dim the lights, fade out the music, and for a few minutes everybody just sits there in silence, some people talking quietly, waiting.

Clearly his tech people have no idea what they're doing. What a disaster. Someone missed a cue. I'm hearing what sounds like bagpipes. Only the sound is coming from behind us. And it's getting louder and louder. Then one of the back doors of the auditorium opens and an actual bagpiper comes in. Have you ever heard bagpipes at close range indoors? Apparently there are two volume levels with the bagpipes: not playing them or, "Hey, I think an airplane just landed in my bedroom" loud. It has this stunning effect on the crowd—we're transfixed. No one is moving. Except Yves. His leg is bouncing like it does when he's really, really amped. What is this like for him, seeing it from the other side?

The bagpipe player has a massive red beard and ponytail, and he's wearing a kilt and hiking boots with bright red socks that have tassels on them. He plays as he walks down the aisle until he makes it to the stage, where he turns to face the crowd, stops playing, and says in a thunderous brogue:

"Ladies and Gentlemen, Lads and Lassies, Enough mucking around. The time has come for Chuck Flannel."

And with that, he walks off stage. As he exits stage left, Chuck Flannel enters stage right.

He has one leg.

I know. I wasn't expecting it either. Chuck Flannel has one leg. And he doesn't have a crutch or walker or cane or fake leg or anything. He hops. But it's not a hop like if you or I were to try and walk on one leg. It's like a glide. Just watching him make his way to the front of the stage so catches me off guard I almost don't want him to say anything because it's taking so much of my energy and headspace just to process that Chuck Flannel has one leg. I look around the room and see that others are doing the same sort of polite gasping thing I'm doing. He stands there for what seems like five minutes (Noll later said it was 37 seconds by his count. Which of course raises the question: Why did Noll know to time it? Do you see now? He was in the CIA for sure.)

And then Chuck Flannel speaks. Only it's more like a bark. He says, and I quote word for word because I will never forget it for as long as I live. He snarls:

"What are you complaining about?"

And you're nailed. You're busted. You're feeling all sorry for him and you can't believe that he makes his way around without a wheelchair or cane or crutches or a fake leg, and your mind is racing with how he must have lost his leg and how much it must have hurt and how tough his life must be and how does he get on the toilet? And you're actually feeling...pity. You're feeling sorry for him. You feel bad for the guy. You're wondering how and why he even gets out of bed in the morning.

All of this is running through your head when he says, "What are you complaining about?" and suddenly you're reminded of all the petty little bitching and moaning that you do all day long about every little tiny thing that doesn't fit into your perfectly convenient plan of how the world is supposed to revolve around you... but this guy, this guy has one less leg than you and he gets up and gets around and doesn't act the slightest bit like a victim. He then launches into this story about how he comes from four generations of Pacific Northwest lumbermen, "men of the woods" he calls them. He shows slides of his great-great and then great- and then grandfather and then his father and then he shows pictures of massive trees, hundreds of feet tall, and he tells about what it was like spending weeks in the woods with these great men of the forest as a young boy, learning the ways of the land. He tells about one day when he was at the top of a massive redwood—"tall as the tallest building"—and his chainsaw slipped from his hand, cut off his leg, and fell to the ground, landing just before his leg did.

He said when his leg hit the ground it made a thud, "like when a watermelon falls off the back of your truck."

He shows a slide of the exact place on the ground where the leg landed. He shows a picture of the mangled chainsaw, lying in a heap not far from where the leg landed. I gag as a little throw-up floods my mouth. The scenes are so visceral and bloody and dramatic I find myself reeling from it. He then tells us what it was like to still be up in the tree. The way he tells it, you feel like you're up there with him. He describes the smell of the leaves and the feel of the bark up against his face and how he had to cling to the trunk of the tree for two hours while they radioed for a helicopter to come rescue him.

I find myself mentally making a list of questions about exactly how these events unfolded: How come he didn't bleed to death or pass out? Why was he up that high all alone? Wasn't there a branch he could have rested on?

But I'm quickly reminded that while I may have questions about the details, this is all trumped by the simple fact he's standing before my very eyes without a leg-there is no leg beneath his left hip.

He tells about how his best friend Rudy Moody happened to be on lunch break walking back into the brush to take a leak when he tripped.

On Chuck's leg.

By the way, only Chuck Flannel would have a best friend named "Rudy Moody."

In the words of Rudy Moody:

"It was obviously Chuck's leg because he's the only dumbass I know who chews Skoal."

Chuck tells us that his tobacco was in the cargo pocket of the pant leg that was sawed off and somehow came out of the pocket and was laying on the ground next to the leg when Rudy Moody almost tripped on it coming back from taking a leak in the woods.

Chuck describes what it was like to cling to that trunk for his dear life, wondering if he would ever see his wife and kids and uncles and brothers—wondering if he would ever bowl again on Tuesday nights at the Strike King or listen to his Elvis Live in Hawaii record or watch his boy wrestle in the state tournament or eat his wife's salmon loaf. Chuck says he clung to that tree because some things are just far too valuable to let go.

He then begins unbuttoning his shirt, and you realize while he's doing it that there is something written on the t-shirt underneath but you can't quite read it until he sticks his chest out and reads it out loud:

"Chuck Flannel: The Original Tree Hugger."

Didn't see that coming.

I know it's a cliché to say this, but "The crowd goes wild!" I've seen people lose it at Yves' talks, but this is different. This cheer has a cathartic quality to it, like it's about something far more significant than what's written on Chuck's shirt.

I look over at Yves and he's got tears in his eyes.

It strikes me that I've never seen Yves show much in the way of emotion. I've seen him make other people cry on a regular basis. I've seen him evoke powerful reactions in others. But the truth is, he's always the strong one. He's the one with the answers. He's the one who leads others through their feelings. His feelings never get in the way.

Chuck then talks about overcoming obstacles and clinging to things because that's what will save your life. And he closes with the question: "Who's waiting for you at home?" I've heard

that sort of thing before but coming from him, it means
something else. Something it didn't before.

As soon as he's done I bolt for the lobby. I have to see if he
has any books. As I enter the lobby I realize that Chuck Flannel
truly is a genius. While we were listening to him, his merch
people had set up long tables perpendicular to the doors piled
high with "Chuck Flannel: The Original Tree Hugger" t-shirts.
Just like he was wearing during his talk. I buy three. The man
ahead of me buys ten, which automatically qualifies him for
the "Chuck Club." One woman behind me asks if there's a
special rate for people who buy one in each color. Chuck is
going to make a lot of money tonight. I must tell Noll. I turn
around and almost run into him—he's standing right there,
taking it all in. We smile at each other. This may be the first
time I have ever seen Noll observing someone beating him at
his own game.

I head back in to talk about it with Yves, and I find him still in
his seat, alone in the row, staring at the stage. I sit down in the
row behind him.

Me: "How about that?"
Yves: "There aren't words."
Me: "How about the classical music at the beginning?
I thought it was sucking the energy out of the room, but it was
a brilliant psychological ploy because it lulled us into this calm,

peaceful state right before his talk. A bit like a trailer park at sunrise on the day of a tornado. They shouldn't call it a talk—they should call it an assault! Unreal. And bagpipes—fookin' bagpipes! 'Enough mucking around. The time has come for Chuck Flannel.' Incredible. They should call it 'The Chuck Flannel Experience.' As in 'The Jimi Hendrix Experience.' And then the slides of where his leg landed!"

Yves: "I almost barfed."

Me: "Me, too!" It was great wasn't it? So inspiring. Did you know he has one leg?

Yves: "No, no clue."

Me: "Totally took me by surprise."

Yves: "Rooster, he's coming from a different place."

Me: "Huh?"

Yves: "He's not coming at it like we do. Like I do. He's doing it for something else. He's in another realm..."

Me: "I'm not following you..."

Yves: "It's hard to explain."

Y

Rooster will never understand. I don't know if I will ever understand. Chuck Flannel makes me not want to speak in public ever again. He makes me want to forget that I ever tried to help anybody do anything. He makes me feel like a sham, a phony, a pretender. I'm sitting here in my seat, clutching my ticket, wondering if I will ever recover from what I just saw.

R

Me: "Let's go, Yves, they're expecting us."
Yves: "Who?"
Me: "Chuck Flannel! Claudia arranged for us to go backstage and meet him."

Y

I can't meet Chuck Flannel! He'll kill me. With one look, he'll kill me and I'll implode from the shame of being a sham. 'Aspirational speaker,' my ass. No, I cannot meet this man with one leg.

R

Is Yves nervous? He looks nervous. I've seen him nervous before speaking to a big crowd, but all we're doing is having a drink with a man whose last name is Flannel. I'm so excited. I can't remember a time I was this thrilled to meet someone.

R

Claudia knocks on the green room door, and it opens and out comes this woman, about my age, and she's holding a clipboard.

And she's beautiful.

Hotness personified: "Hello, are you Claudia? I'm Phoebe, Chuck's daughter, everybody calls me Feeb."
Claudia: "Yes, Feeb, great to meet you. Thanks so much for arranging for us to come back and meet your dad."
Feeb: "Oh he loves making new friends after a gig. You'll see."
Claudia: "This is my husband Noll and this is Yves and this is Rooster."
Me: "Hi Feeb."
Feeb: "Hi...Rooster. Great name. Did your parents give you that?"
Me: "No, I traded Donald in for it."
Feeb: "That's funny, Donald."
Me: "Rooster will be fine, thanks."

And so we go in the dressing room and there sits Chuck Flannel in a Lazy Boy, one of those recliners with the lever on

the side that raises up the footrest. He's got a Mike's Hard
Lemonade in one hand and his shoes are off and there's a dog
laying on the floor next to him. A big dog. Maybe a Great Dane
or a Mastiff. I have been in a thousand dressing rooms, and I
have never seen a Lazy Boy in one. Or a dog. Let alone both at
the same time.

Feeb: "Dad, Yves Green is here. And this is Claudia who does
his PR and Noll who does his merch and this is Rooster, and
Rooster, well, actually, I don't know what Rooster does, what
do you do?"
Me: "I'm in charge of logistics." I shake Chuck's hand. Or more
accurately, Chuck crushes my hand.
Chuck: "Logistics. What kind of job title is that?"
Me: "Well, details, arrangements, sorting things out..."
Chuck: "You mean Wingman! That's what Feeb does for me!
She's my Wingman. She makes it all happen and when she
does it well, no one even realizes just how much work it took
to pull it off. People don't even notice it because everything
runs so smoothly. That's what you do?"
Me: "Yes, exactly." Oh man, Chuck gets it. No one has ever
understood how hard my job is and how the better I do it the
less anyone notices. It's only when there isn't a car waiting by
the back door or the food isn't hot and on time or the hotel
reservations aren't made that anybody says anything. Chuck is
my new hero.

Chuck: "And you, Yves Green, sit down, get a drink, and tell me about yourself!"

Yves clears his throat—is he actually nervous? Yves?

Yves: "Well, I've been an aspirational speaker for about twenty years now—"
Chuck: "A what?"
Yves: "An aspirational speaker. Kind of like a motivational speaker. I try to help people understand what it is they aspire to and how they can get there."
Chuck: "You light fires."
Yves: "Excuse me?"
Chuck: "You light fires. That's what you do. You light fires under people. You inspire them. You create in them a dissatisfaction with the life they have settled for and a longing for something better."
Yves: "Well, yes, that's what I try to do—"
Claudia: "Yves, don't be humble. You are a fire lighter! You are the pyromaniac of people's souls!"
Chuck: "That's what I'm talking about Sister! You're on it, Claudia! I have no tolerance for all that formal language about titles and descriptions. Whenever people refer to me as a motivational speaker, I want to gag. I just go around lighting fires!"
Yves: "You really lit it up tonight—that was great. Really great. I have so many questions..."

R

So off Chuck and Yves go into conversation, Claudia and Noll head out to meet Chuck's merch people, which leaves me talking with the clipboard goddess.

Me: "So, you run your dad's operation?"
Feeb: "Yep, for part of the year, the rest of the year I work with a nonprofit teaching kids how to manage money."
Me: "Like bank accounts and checkbooks?"
Feeb: "No, much more basic. We teach them about innovation and creativity and how to take resources to make things grow. It's great. I love it."
Me: "And then you hit the road with your dad…"

I am having a very difficult time keeping this conversation going. I am so in to this woman. Oh man. I am fidgeting and trying not to but the more I tell myself to calm down the more I fidget. I think my face is red. She is so confident and organized and solid and hot. So hot. I can't stop staring. Whatever she just said I don't remember it at all, not one word. I wasn't listening. I was busy standing in awe.

"Hey, Chicken!"
Feeb: "Dad, it's Rooster."
Chuck: "Hey Rooster, if you even think about making eyes at my daughter, I'll kick your shiny white ass so hard your shout will be a squeak. Got it?"

Yves: "I'd love to see that."

I freeze. I blush. And then Chuck bursts out laughing. "I'm just messing with you. But seriously, what kind of a name is Rooster? And while I'm at it, what kind of name is Yves? How do you spell it? Eve? Isn't that a girl's name?"

Yves: "No, it's spelled Y-V-E-S."
Chuck: "So you got a girl's name but it's spelled like a boy's?"
Yves: "It's French. My mom lived in Paris before she married and—"
Chuck: "French? Those people clearly can't name a child to save their lives, but I'll forgive them because of all they've done for kissing and toast and potatoes.

I laugh out loud at that.
Chuck: "You think that's funny, Rooster? I do, too. I think we could be friends."
Me: "Yes, sir, I think we could." Did I really call him "sir"?

Yves (who finally seems to be relaxing): "So Chuck, how many days a year are you out?"
Chuck: "In the woods?"
Yves: "No, traveling. On the road. Speaking and signing and promoting—"
Chuck: "Promoting? I haven't done a day of promoting. I do a week or two of nights like this, and then I go home for a couple

of months and then I might go back out and do a few more,
but only if it works for us."

Yves: "For us?"

Chuck: "Yes, my family, friends, kids. It has to work for all of us
or there's no point."

Yves: "But what about building your brand?"

Chuck: "Building my brand? What the—? Why V's, you got
fungus growing on both sides of your trunk boy! What are you
talking about? Building my brand, I couldn't give two shots off
a monkey's ass about building my brand!"

Yves: "But how do you make sure your name recognition is
increasing and sales are growing?"

Chuck: "Eve, my good Frenchman, there are very few things
you can actually control."

Yves: "But what if people stop coming to hear you or buying
your shirts?"

Chuck: "Let me tell you what I'll do. You know that tree? The
one I clung too when I lost my leg? I went back there after I
got out of the hospital and I cut that sonofabitch down and I
built a table with the wood, a big, long, wide table. We have
meals around that table. I gather all of the people I love the
most, and we eat and we sing and we tell stories and we laugh
and we cry and we enjoy...it's about eating long meals with
those you love the most and swimming in a lake and taking a
nap under a tree in the middle of the day. This—tickets and t-
shirts and crowds and hotels—this is just the frosting, my
good Frenchman.

Yves: "The frosting?"

Chuck: "The frosting. It's the bonus, the extra. The part that makes you say to yourself, 'I can't believe I get to do this.' But it's not the point. It's not the cake. What happens if the crowds stop coming? What happens if I run out of things to say? This isn't where I find out who I am. It's where I share who I am. This does not define me. It's the frosting. And if it falls off, I'm still enjoying a fine piece of cake."

Yves: "So you only do this a few weeks out of the year?"

Chuck: "I can only handle it that much. Eating out is death. How can you eat food when you don't know where it came from? I speak for a week or so, and then I go back to my life. I appear, and then I disappear. If you don't go up on the mountain for a while, how are you ever going to bring down any tablets?"

Yves: "Tablets?"

Me: "It's a Jewish thing...Moses and the Ten—"

Yves: "A Jewish thing?"

Chuck: "No wonder people feel disconnected from their lives. They don't know where their tomatoes were grown! They don't know the maid who made their bed in the hotel. They don't know the name of the taxi driver who drove them from the airport...If you don't know those things, you don't know nothin'!"

R

Chuck is totally giving it to Yves. And he's taking it. It seems pretty serious what they're talking about. But I have much more important work in front of me: "So, how'd you end up working for your dad?"

Feeb: "I'd just graduated from college when he lost his leg, and I spent about a month sitting by his bed, talking to him and holding his hand and telling him how much I love him. Our family is like that—we say exactly what we're thinking. People from around the hospital kept stopping by to check on him and make sure he was doing okay but he would always end up inspiring them. So on the day he left the hospital I organized a farewell ceremony. The doctors and nurses were taking turns giving speeches about what an honor it was to care for my dad when he jumped up out of his wheelchair, grabbed the microphone, and gave a spontaneous talk about how he didn't LOSE his leg, he GAVE it to the earth. He took over and turned it into a revival-pep-rally-group-therapy-session. One of the nurses asked me afterwards if he could come give that exact talk to the monthly meeting of all the nurses in the hospital, which I convinced him to do, and that led to more a few more gigs and every time it was incredible. One led to the next and before I knew it, I was standing in front of a plastic container of little carrots, telling my story to a man named Rooster, who is not allowed to make eyes at me or my dad will kick his "shiny white ass."

R

My knees wobble. This woman owns me.

Chuck: "Well this has been a smashing time, Gentlemen—you, too, Claudia. But now I must get out of my chair and go lay my head down in a hotel somewhere."

Yves: "That's your chair?"

Chuck: "Of course. Top of the line."

Me: "From home?"

Feeb: "Yes, he insists on taking it with us on the road. As well as Roger, his dog."

Yves: "You take this chair and your dog wherever you go?"

Chuck: "A little piece of home wherever I am."

Me: "The chair? Your dog is the size of a small horse! How do you get away with that with the airlines?"

Feeb: "Would you say no to a man with one leg?"

R

It's an hour later and we are sitting in the bar of our hotel, waiting for Yves to join us so we can do another round of applications. I have only one thought: and that thought carries a clipboard.

Noll: "Chuck was something else."

Claudia: "I thought he was sweet. And his daughter—what an angel!"

Noll: "That might not be the word Rooster would use."

Me: "What? Who, Feeb? Yeah, she was nice I guess..."
Loll: "Please. You were whipped from the moment you laid eyes on her clipboard."
Claudia: "Oh my, so there is a heart in there somewhere, this is new..."
Me: "Can we just read the first application?"
Yves: (Who's been lost in thought the whole time...) "Yes, let's get to the applications."

We do this for a while, taking turns until Yves says with mild irritation: "How come so many of them mention how hard they work? This guy makes a point to let us know that he hasn't taken a vacation—and this, where is it? Here: remember this one from earlier? Merle McCollough wrote, 'I rarely see my family. Maybe one dinner a week. That's how committed I am to being the best.' Does this bother anyone else?"

Claudia: "Well, they listen to you."
Yves: "Explain."
Noll: "They pay attention. These are your hardcore followers, and they don't miss a thing. You have demonstrated a way of life that they're seeking to emulate."
Me: "Seeking to emulate?"
Claudia: "Yes, they want to be like him. And they go to the website and see his travel schedule and they hear him talk about how much it takes to get to the top and so they do it—

they work long hours and they're rarely home and they give everything they have…"

Yves: "Here's a perfect example of what I'm talking about: 'To give you an idea of how serious I am, I haven't taken a vacation in three years. My wife asked me the other day: can't we splurge just once and go somewhere beautiful and put our feet up and not have a care in the world? And you know what I said to her? I said, 'Honey, you drive a new car, you get to pick out whatever clothes you want, and the kids are going to college because we've saved up plenty, and look at this house. What more could you ask for? And where does it come from? Me working. That's just the cost of having a wonderful life.'"

Yves looks around at each of us, and when no one comments, he says, "It doesn't sit right with me."

Noll: "Well, let's wrap it up for the night. We got almost fifty done tonight, and that, my friends, is progress…and progress sits well with you, doesn't it Yves? Rooster, what time do we fly in the morning?"

Me: "Ten. Breakfast at seven. Shuttle at eight."

R

I am driving home from the airport. In my new GTI. It still smells like the day I bought it. Is new car smell the actual smell of the car itself, or is it a smell, like a spray or something, that they coat the inside of the car with after they make it?

Because if you could buy it in a can or sprayer, I would. This car is joy. I've owned it for a month, but I've only driven it a couple of times. I have three days ahead with time to kill. I will drive my new car. I will own the road.

Y

I am driving home from the airport, like I have done hundreds of times. I have been gone for thirteen days. I have slept in nine different beds. I have talked to eleven thousand people. I will be home for three days before we go out for six, then we'll be home for two, then out for ten. Usually when I'm driving home I'm thinking about the next trip, the next talks, wondering what the crowds will be like, looking ahead to the next adventure. But today, today I think thoughts I have never thought before driving home from the airport.

I don't want to go back out. I want to stay home. I don't want to come back to the airport in three days. I don't want to check in and get my ticket. I don't want to take off my belt and shoes and stand there in my socks waiting to go through the metal detector. I don't want to get on another plane. I don't want to sleep in another hotel bed. I don't want to order another meal.

I pull in the driveway and notice the lawn hasn't been mowed.

I vaguely remember Khloe saying she had gotten into an argument with the lawn service people—apparently, that hasn't been resolved. Those are the kind of details I don't ever think about. She takes care of them, I am ignorant. I walk into the house—my house/our house—and I notice things I've never noticed before. Charis' shoes. Lots of them. Bottled water. A stack of mail. A pile of Big Girl shirts in the garage. Khloe is gone somewhere, and I assume Charis is at school. It is the middle of the day and the house is really big and really empty.

R

I have a routine when I return home from a trip. I organize the mail. I clean my apartment. I go for a run. I head to my favorite pub for dinner. I watch a movie. I start working on the next trip.

Y

When I return home from a trip, I have a little routine. I put my clothes away. I take a run. I read my emails from people who heard me on the last trip. They're grateful and kind and sometimes a little creepy but that's just because they're so appreciative. I usually spend hours doing this. I bask in these emails. They're the reward for all the work.

I put my clothes away. I take a run. I read my emails but I'm done in five minutes. They're kind and appreciative and gushing, but it doesn't mean what it used to. I go outside and stand in the backyard. The lawn needs to be mowed. This bothers me. That's better. There is something about a fresh cut lawn that is so earthy. Real. And the smell. On my fingers, in the air, the green ring around the sole of my shoes. I am sitting on a chair in the middle of my backyard and I feel like a king. My wife's home…

Khloe: "Did you see which of them it was? The short one with the giant headphones or the older one with white hair? Because if it was the older one—"
Me: "Which of them who did what?"
Khloe: "Mowed the lawn."
Me: "I did."
Khloe: "You did?"
Me: "I did."
Khloe: "You mowed the lawn?"
Me: "Yes."
Khloe: "With what mower?"
Me: "Our new mower. Want to see it? It's in the garage…"
Khloe: "You bought a lawnmower?"
Me: "I got a sweet deal—on sale."
Khloe: "How do you even know how to start it?"
Me: "Al, the sales guy, gave me a demo. Turns out he's a big fan. He actually followed me home and showed me how to use it. All I had to do was sign a book for him."
Khloe: "Are you okay?"
Me: "It's good to see you, too."

K
You need to understand that even when Yves is home, he's
not really home. He watches television, he sleeps, he works
out, he sits in front of the computer and reads fan mail. He
eats with us. He essentially watches us live our life. And then
he leaves again. Yves' life is out there, not here. The few days
we do see him, it's not like he enters into the flow of our lives.
He's good about going to dance recitals and listening to me
tell about my day and he'll do the dishes, but he's a shell of a
man. He gives everything he has while he's gone, and when
he's home, he recovers. It's been like this for years. I could
complain but what would be the point? I'm used to it and I've
learned to have my own life.

A long time ago I gave up asking questions about whether or
not this is the life I planned for us—our life. What good is
planning when it's going to take it's own course anyway?
Obviously, any counselor off the street could point out that Big
Girl is what I do in the absence of my husband—I get that. But
I love it. And I get to meet lots of people and I have a full life
and our daughter doesn't seem to be suffering. So that's what
my life is.

But this, mowing the lawn, this is new.

Y

When the salesman, Al, was giving the demonstration, he
talked about crosscutting. He explained that you mow in
straight lines one way, and then you mow the lawn again in
rows perpendicular to the rows you just made so the lawn gets
a checkerboard effect. Like on golf courses. I actually got a
little thrill thinking about crosscutting. I'll have to work up to it.

K

And then at dinner he starts asking questions. Questions he
never asks about—he has staff who handle the details for him.
He doesn't even notice the details. But tonight, tonight he
wouldn't stop. I thought Charis was going to flip when he
asked her about her homework. She kept looking at him like
he's an alien. He's simply never had the energy to get that
involved with her life. He loves her and she loves him and
that's about it. But I have to keep in mind: he's home for three
days and then he's out again. Three days. What could possibly
change in three days?

Y

I'm sitting in a chair in the backyard at nine in the morning.
I gaze upon my lawn as a king would look out over his
kingdom. I feel nothing but pride and joy. It looks great, and I
did that. What am I going to do today? I don't want to meet

with Rooster and go over details for the upcoming trip. I don't
want to read emails. I don't want to work on another book. I
don't have anything inspiring to say today. I want to grow
tomatoes.

R

So last night I finally watched Fight Club. I've been a Fincher
fan for a while and Edward Norton? Is there a better actor? I
don't know how many times people have told me I have to see
it, but as soon as too many people like something I get this
contrarian thing where I decide I'm not going to watch it-
apparently I think I'm making some sort of point about how I
can think for myself and I don't need people telling me what
I'm going to like. So last night—after 10 years of holding out—I
gave in and watched Fight Club. There's this scene where
Edward Norton is in his apartment and he talks about the IKEA
catalogue and I get the chills because he has the exact same
living room in the movie that I have in real life. The point is that
his life has no meaning and of course my life does, but still the
living room furniture haunted me. Literally, it haunted me. I had
this dream that I can remember this morning down to the last
detail. I was in IKEA, shopping for a coffee table and there was
this shelf with a box on it and I reached up to pull it down and
when I did, tons of coffee tables crashed down on me but it
didn't hurt. And then a television, a big plasma screen landed
on me and then bath towels, which did hurt—how odd that

pieces of furniture didn't hurt but bath towels did, and then
silverware and curtains and couches and then pillows, only the
pillows had the VW logo on them, and it's all pouring down on
me like I'm at the bottom of a waterfall but only some of it
hurts while the rest just bounces off and this dream went on
and on and on, all of this stuff burying me. I think it's quite
clear what the dream was about: don't watch a movie just
because everybody recommends it.

Y

I'm on my knees in the yard on the side of the house, when I
get the feeling I'm being watched. I get up and turn around,
and there's this kid standing there, watching me.

Me: "Can I help you?"
Him: "Is Charis home?"
Me: "No. She said something this morning about an art project
after school."
Him: "Could you tell her Greg stopped by?"
Me: "Sure."
Him: "Thanks."

And then, as he walks away, he turns around and says, "You're
doing it wrong—see how the overhang from your garage is
shading the place you're working in right now? You want them
exposed to the sun this time of the day..."

And so I find myself discussing the angle of the sun and how deep to dig and proper placement with Greg Dodge, the boy who fancies my daughter. He shows me a better place and then offers to help, and we start talking and I find out that he has dyslexia and he loves tennis and his favorite rapper is Jay Z and he once got busted for toilet papering his neighbor's house.

K

What? Charis and I are pulling in the driveway, and I see two rear-ends by the side door. One belongs to Yves, and when we get out of the car, I discover that the other belongs to a high-school kid. Charis looks confused but then she starts smiling and fidgeting at the same time...

Me: "Charis, do you know him?"
Charis: "That's Greg Dodge."
Me: "How does your dad know Greg Dodge?"
Charis: "I don't know if I want to know."

R

I haven't heard from Yves yet. Usually by now we're plotting and scheming and debriefing and talking about the next trip and all of the places we're going to go and crowds he'll speak to...but so far, nothing. Not even an email. He's always called by day two.

C

Oh. My. God. Like I could totally bury myself in the earth next to whatever it is they're planting. Greg and my Dad are working together in our yard, and I'm supposed to say hello like this is normal? Nightmare! And then my mom, as always, takes charge...

Khloe: "And what are you doing, gentlemen?"
The two of them stand up and brush dirt off their knees.
Yves: "Planting tomatoes. Greg here has some serious tomato skills."
Khloe: "Hi Greg, I'm Charis' mom and Mr. Green's wife."
Greg: "Hello, Nice to meet you. I just stopped by to see Charis, and it seemed like maybe Mr. Green needed... uh, a little assistance getting started on his project here..."
Khloe: "Well, yes, this is an interesting little project Mr. Green has started here. I'm curious what made him want to plant tomatoes."
Yves: "I was in the backyard this morning, and all of a sudden, I realized that a man ought to grow his own vines..."

C

I think my dad may be losing it. Last night he asked me what we're learning in American History class and what's on my iTunes and when's my next recital, and then today, he's planting tomatoes with Greg. Thank God, he's only around for another day. What else could he possibly do in one day?

Y

I have an idea. A good idea…

Me: "I have an idea. Let's all go out for dinner together. Greg, can you come? Charis, you pick the restaurant…"

Later, as I sit on the edge of my bed, not a hotel bed but my bed, taking off my socks, I realize that I have a massive pit in my stomach—too many fish tacos? No, it's been there. I hear Khloe in the bathroom brushing her teeth, and then she says, "Nice stunt tonight—inviting Greg to dinner."

Me: "You think so?"
Khloe: "You sure know how to put your daughter through the ringer. She didn't know whether to crawl under the table or give you a hug for caring."
Me: "Why would she want to crawl under the table?"
Khloe: "Think about it from her perspective: Her dad is home for three days in which he mows the lawn, plants tomatoes,

doesn't appear to do any of the work which she usually sees
him do, and then he invites a boy she likes to dinner with the
family.”

Me: “So? I enjoyed it.”

Khloe: “Yes, you enjoyed it. But you're not acting like you. It's
strange for your daughter. It's strange for your wife. We don't
know what do with you...”

Me: “Can I share something with you?”

Khloe: “Yes, unless it involves purchasing lawn ornaments,
because I have to draw the line somewhere.”

Me: “Ha ha. No, this is serious. I have a massive pit in my
stomach, and I've had it since I got home. And it won't go
away. And it's getting worse by the minute. Tonight at dinner,
when I was telling Greg about how when Charis was three she
ate that stick of butter? Just telling that story made it get
exponentially worse, like my insides were going to cave in.”

Khloe: “Should you see a doctor?”

Me: “Khloe, I don't want to go.”

Khloe: “Go where?”

Me: “I don't want to go back out on the road. I don't want to
give any talks. I don't want to sign any books. I don't have
anything to say.”

Khloe: “How long have you been feeling this way?”

Me: “On the last trip, I had this moment right after getting off
stage when I had no energy. I literally had to sit down in the
hall and just...be. It was like something deep in my bones got

unplugged from the wall. I can't really describe it. I can always rally, I can always find energy to keep going, I never give up...”
Khloe: “Well, let's plan a vacation and get you some rest.”
Me: “No, no, no—that's the problem. This isn't that kind of tired. I haven't done any work for these past few days and it's gotten worse. Whatever it is, it won't get fixed with a week at the beach. It's like my soul needs a vacation. Or my brain. Or my heart. But it can't be a vacation, because the whole time you're not working you know that in just a few days you're going to be right back working where you were when you left. That's the problem—this isn't like that. This is about space.”
Khloe: “Space?”
Me: “Space. Time. Distance. I need to leave my life and see it from outside of it so I can see why this is happening to me.”
Khloe: “You want to leave your life. Would you like to change your name as well?”
Me: “No, no, it's not about you or our life or our house or... well it is, but it isn't. I need space to figure out what's happening inside me. And if I get that space, but five days later I have to go back to being the Yves Green that we all know—”
Khloe: “—and love—”
Me: “—and love—yes, of course. If I get some space from being the Yves Green we all know and love, but then I have to go back to being him a few days later, then the space doesn't mean anything. Does that make any sense?”
Khloe: “Not really. The only thing I know for sure about you is that you always keep going. That's always been the one

consistent thing about you—you never quit and you never give up and you never say you're tired. You always have something more."

Me: "But that's it. I don't have something more. Whatever that thing is, that energy or will or drive, whatever it is, I don't have it anymore."

Khloe: "It's gone?"

Me: "It's gone."

Khloe: "Have you told Noll?"

Me: "Kind of."

Khloe: "Can we talk about this more in the morning?"

Y

I sleep like a baby.

K

I toss and turn most of the night. My husband always makes sense and is always predictable and never fails to be on time. I have never heard Yves confused or not making sense. He always figures everything out and then speaks. Space? Distance? Tired? At one point he said it was like something "deep in his bones got unplugged from the wall." Huh?

Y

At breakfast:

Charis: "Dad, Greg texted me last night to tell me he thinks you're one of the raddest dads he knows."

Me: "He did?"

Charis: "Yep, right after we dropped him off."

Me: "Khloe, did you hear that? Greg thinks I'm rad..."

Charis: "Calm down—he also said you're a crap gardener."

After breakfast, after Charis has left for school:

Khloe: "I was thinking about what you said last night."

Me: "Good."

Khloe: "And I want to know how serious you are. Were you just venting because it felt good, or were you being serious? Because if you mean it, if you don't want to go back on the road, there will be consequences. So I can listen and try to help you, but there are people who make their living from you being Yves Green."

My phone rings and I look to see who it is.

Me: "It's Rooster."

Khloe: "I think you should answer it and tell him what you've been telling me."

Me: "Hey, Rooster!"

Rooster: "Yves, what's going on?"

Me: "Oh the usual, just having a chat with the president of Big Girl Lemonade."

Rooster: "Tell her I said hi. Listen, I'm free this morning if you want to get at it."

Me: "Yeah...about that...listen, Rooster, I'm rethinking some stuff...I'm—"

Rooster: "What are you rethinking? Because I've got a ton of ideas about your Blue Ocean thing. I think the "aspirational" word is a bit dodgy, but your idea? I think there's something there. I did a ton of reading yesterday on it, and I looked through some case studies—"

Me: "No, Rooster, I'm sorry, I wasn't clear. I'm not sure I want to go back out. I'm rethinking—"

Rooster: "Back out? Like tomorrow morning? You don't want to go?"

Me: "Well, it isn't that I don't want to...I'm not sure I'm able to... I'm probably not making much sense..."

And just when I began to fear that I had dug a hole that I would never be able to dig myself out of, Khloe hits speaker on my phone.

Khloe: "Rooster, Khloe here. I just put you on speaker."

Rooster: "Hi, Khloe."

Khloe: "Rooster, look, here's the situation: Yves is going through some sort of thing. I don't quite know what it is, but he isn't making much sense, and whatever it is, he doesn't seem to be terribly fired up about hopping on a plane with you tomorrow morning and going wherever it is you're going."

Rooster: "But we have commitments and schedules and we've signed contracts—"

Khloe: "I don't know if I'm being clear enough here, so let me tell you how serious this is. Rooster, Yves mowed the lawn two days ago."

Rooster: "He mowed the lawn?"

Khloe: "See what I mean? And then yesterday, he planted tomatoes."

Rooster: "Khloe, quit messing with me."

Khloe: "And do you want to know what he was wearing yesterday when I pulled into the driveway and I found him planting tomato vines? He was wearing sweatpants."

Rooster: "Sweatpants? You're making this up."

Me: "Rooster, I have dirt under my fingernails. Actual dirt. Yesterday I could hold my hand up to my face and smell the earth. My sweatpants are dirty. Rooster, my sweatpants are dirty. How awesome is that?"

R

Yes, he has lost it. It is now a fact.

Y

Khloe: "Have I made my point?"

Rooster: "I still don't get it."

Me: "Me neither, but at least—"

Rooster: "Yves, I really don't get it. Your third book was called Enough with the Sweatpants—"

Me: "Yes, I know that, I wrote it."

Rooster: "No, but listen: You talked about how sweatpants are the ultimate in giving up, that when a person wears sweatpants around they've essentially given in to the life of a slob. You mocked sweatpants. You asked people if they've ever seen a picture of someone who changed the world wearing sweatpants. You invited people to send pictures in to the website of them burning their sweatpants, and now I'm hearing that you've been wearing sweatpants."

Me: "Actually, you know that pair that we bought for the photo shoot for the book? I kept them in the basement, and when I needed something to wear for my tomato planting, I went and found them. And they fit! I've actually been wearing that exact pair. Ironic, isn't it?"

Rooster: "Ironic is not the word I would use. Deeply disturbing is more like it. Yves, something is up with you and I don't get it."

Khloe: "Let's do this: You call Claudia and Noll and all of you come for dinner tonight and we'll talk this whole thing through. Six o'clock work for you?"

Y

After the call with Rooster, I'm thinking maybe this won't be so
hard for everyone to understand. Then I ask Khloe:
"So what are you thinking for dinner? Should I grill something
— do we even have a grill? Maybe Al sells grills and could help
me."
Khloe: "Yves look at me. I don't know what's happening to
you. But we have a life here, me and Charis, and it works for
us. And it works for us because you fit in a certain place in our
life. Now I am perfectly happy to be your loving supportive
wife and walk beside you through whatever this is you're going
through, but you need to get serious help sorting this out.
Make a plan and get some help—now."

R

I hang up and my brain starts to spin. Possible scenarios are
flashing in my mind faster than I can take in the details.
Will I have to get a new job? Is Yves going mental? Like those
geniuses who can't take it and they crack? Will we get sued if
he doesn't show? And of course the worst nightmare of all: Is
there a chance I will end up living back in my parents'
basement in my childhood bedroom in Ohio, which my dad
reminded me last Christmas, "hasn't been touched since you
left in case your little deal with the motivational fella falls
through and you don't want to end up in a van down by the

river." Which he thought was quite clever. Shoot me now before I ever have to move back home.

I do what anybody would do in my shoes: I get in my car and drive really fast for a while. The new car smell calms my nerves.

Y

I have several hours to make a plan. I sit in the backyard, in a chair on my freshly cut grass. I am desperate for a next step. I have an idea.

Me: "Lou, Yves here."
Lou: "Yves, heard you killed it at the baseball thing—they're already hounding me about next year."
Me: "Great, listen, I need a favor. What was the name of that singer you were working with, the one from Austin who took a little break?"
Lou: "Bubba Love?"
Me: "Yeah, Bubba Love, I remember you telling me she had some problem with her dad and went to some estate where they—"
Lou: "Of course, Hesed House."
Me: "Hesed House? What happened to her?"
Lou: "That's where she went. She signed her first contract, recorded her first album, it went top ten, she did her first tour

and in some city, I think it was Tulsa, her dad shows up
outside the venue, telling everybody who he is. Here she is
twenty-two, she's never met her dad, but as soon as she's rich
and famous, he shows up. Absolutely traumatized her. He
confronted her outside her bus at one in the morning, told her
he'd come to rescue her like he'd always planned."
Me: "Is he nuts?"
Lou: "Of course. So she calls me in the middle of the night,
sobbing, saying she needed some space."
Me: "And you recommended Hesed?"
Lou: "Yep, I'd heard about it from a friend who sent his brother
there, real uppity sort of CEO of some dot.com who worked so
hard in the nineties that by his early thirties the doctor told him
he had no adrenaline left in his body—he literally blew his
adrenal glands. My friend said Hesed helped him learn a whole
new way to live. Apparently when he first got there he had
problems falling asleep lying down."
Me: "I don't get it…"
Lou: "He had slept in his office for so many years, he got to
the point where he could only fall asleep on his desk.
Now I'm a bit skeptical of treatment centers where they have
you tell your story and 'unpack your past' and all that sort of
thing, but in his case, it worked. Came out a new man. So
that's how I first heard about it and when Bubba was in
trouble, I knew she needed more than a vacation. She needed
serious professional help to work through some of that family
stuff. Those waters can be mighty murky. Ambition and drive

and work and all that-poor girl had been working herself silly
and when it finally starts to pay off for her, she's too tired to
enjoy it."
Me: "So she liked this place?"
Lou: "She says to this day the H saved her life—I say anything
that costs a thousand dollars a day should save your life."
Me: "She claims it saved her life?"
Lou: "She does, but that may be a bit exaggerated. This is,
after all, the young lady who wrote the song, "Stalker for Your
Love."
Me: "Right…Thanks, Lou. That helps. I was just curious."
Lou: "Curious for who?"
Me: "A friend of Khloe's. I vaguely remembered you telling me
about Bubba and figured I could at least pass along the name
of this place."
Lou: "Oh, and, for what it's worth, the food there is amazing.
When I visited Bubba there it was Mexican night. Incredible.
I'd pretend to be crazy and check myself in there just for the
green chile."

Y

Within seconds I am on the Hesed House website. I'm
expecting the sort of new age thing that affirms all of my
stereotypes about people who cover themselves with hot
rocks and chant to get their vibrations right, but instead the
place looks professional. There's a list of staff and it's one

Ph.D. after another and "Dr." so and so and this person is a
recognized expert in such and such...They use words I don't
get like "holistic" and "neurofeedback" but beyond that, it's
obviously legit. There's a tab labeled "CONFIDENTIALITY"
which I click. It reads:

"We take very seriously the private, confidential nature of each
person's journey. While we are very proud of the work that we
do here, we acknowledge that among some people the terms
'therapeutic' and 'health center' aren't understood in their
proper context. We therefore find it totally appropriate if any of
our clients choose to check in under an assumed name."

Khloe comes through the room while I'm on the site: "When
was the last time you shaved?"
Me: "Three days."
Khloe: "I like it."
There's another tab, labeled "COST." I click it. Lou was right, a
thousand dollars a day.
Me (to Khloe in the other room): "Remember how you said I
needed to get some help? I have a plan."
Khloe: "Talk to me."

Y

Dinner is tense. Claudia is chatty and Khloe is uber-hostess and Noll is wearing some sort of shirt-sweater vest combo that I wouldn't be caught dead in but it works on him. And Rooster has a sunburn, which he explained by saying, "There's a reason why they call it a SUNroof..."

But we know each other too well to put this off for very long.

Me: "Thanks for coming, There's a few things I need to tell you. I'm realizing that the EXPLODE weekend is going to take a ton out of me—more than I had expected. Being home these few days and thinking about that event, which is only a few weeks away—"
Rooster: "Seven."
Me: "Yes, thank you, seven weeks away. I can do all of these events between now and then, and we can stick to the schedule and travel all over and do what we've been planning on doing, but it will be time and energy I could be spending preparing for the EXPLODE talks—see what I mean?"
Noll: "So what are you proposing?"
Me: "I'm proposing that I cancel everything between now and then and do nothing but prepare for it. I could even go away to really think and prepare. We all know it will be great, but what if it was incredible? Think about it. I've never done anything like it-what if I were to take the time to do nothing but focus on this one event?"

Rooster: "And what would we tell the people who think you're coming to their event between now and then?"

Me: "That's a bit sticky. But what if we agreed to find replacements for me? What if we told them I couldn't make it because of scheduling conflicts—"

Claudia: "Isn't that lying?"

Me: "I don't think so. I think we've learned that this EXPLODE thing is bigger than we ever anticipated and we're having to adjust— people will understand that."

Rooster: "And what will we—me and Claudia and Noll—what will we do for those weeks?"

Khloe: "Yves and I have been talking about that. We want to give you a paid vacation. You'll get your paycheck like you always do."

Noll: "You want to give us a month of paid vacation?"

Me: "Yes. You deserve it."

Claudia: "Is there something else going on here Yves, something you need to tell us that you aren't?"

Me: "Not really...I'm just realizing that it's time to take my game to a whole new level. We've done things a certain way for years now, and I think we're evolving, graduating, new worlds are opening up for us. I don't know exactly what it looks like, but we've put in our time, haven't we? We've earned the opportunity to rethink some things. This is a like a pit stop in a long race. I'm just charging my batteries before the big one..."

Rooster: "I think I kind of get it. You want me to make about fifty totally awkward phone calls telling people you're backing out of your commitment to come and speak at their event, and then you want me to find your replacement and then, when that's done, you want me to find something to do for a month and then you want to come back from wherever it is you're doing and walk into EXPLODE with everything taken care of like you were never gone."

This produces a bit of silence. We each stare at anything but each other, trying to figure out who says what next.

Khloe: "Yes, Rooster, that's exactly what we want you to do."

More silence.

Finally Rooster speaks: "Okay. let's do this. I don't get it. But let's do this."

I feel relief that I cannot begin to put in words.

Me: "Thank you for everything. I don't know what I'd do without you all."

And with that, we toast. To what, we don't know, it just seems like the right thing to do.

Y

I am standing in the driveway of the H—that's what insiders
call it, "the H"—a bag in hand, watching the taxi drive away. I
am in new territory, land I have not visited. And I'm not just
speaking metaphorically. The H is in the middle of nowhere
Arizona. Serious desert nowhere. So far out that the driver said
when it does rain, which is a couple of times a year, the roads
get washed out. Which is why I have to walk up what looks like
a mile-long driveway. It rained last week. I am wearing
sweatpants. I have grown a beard. I haven't had a haircut in a
long time. I've gained a bit of weight. I am wearing sandals.

After that dinner at our house, things kind of fell apart for me. I
had trouble getting up in the morning, I lost the drive to do
much of anything. I never mowed the lawn again. Once I had a
plan, an escape, I let my guard down. And it's been horrible. I
went to see a movie in the middle of the day because Khloe
said I was depressing her sitting around the house watching
her work. There was this scene at the end—I can't remember
the name of the film, but I'll never forget this scene—where the
guy tells his daughter that he's just a tired old man, and it
made me bawl like a baby. Here I am, all alone in the middle of
the theatre crying uncontrollably. When it was over, I went out
the fire exit just so I wouldn't have to see anybody. It's only
been a few weeks and yet I feel like another person, like I
barely know that man who takes the stage and blows the roof
off.

R

I often wonder if Yves was telling the truth. I have never caught even the slightest whiff of a lie coming from him, but that whole speech at dinner doesn't sit well with me. I think it may be because of the weirdness that preceded it—sitting in that chair in the back hallway and not saying anything, refusing to come out and sign books. It's like there were these little signs that something was up and then at his house he gives us this speech about how he's more on top of things than ever and he's actually going to take things "to a new level."

It sounded fake.

Like he wasn't just trying to convince us of something—he was trying to convince himself of something. But Khloe wouldn't put up with fake and she definitely wouldn't go along with a lie, so that makes me think he was genuine.

Y

The H is beautiful. As I walk up the driveway I see the main building for the first time. It's white and stucco and spreads out in all sorts of directions—kind of low and sprawling—and it's built up against a mountain so the back drop is breath-taking, and there are little houses, more like huts or cabins, made of the same white stucco that dots the side of the mountain, about twenty or thirty yards apart. It's quiet, and there are cactus everywhere.

And the air, the air is that dry, desert kind that makes you feel healthy just inhaling. I have this thought that I have landed on another planet and I'm about knock on the door of the first house I come across...

R

I made 43 phone calls telling 43 people that Yves Green wouldn't be able to make it to their event because of "scheduling conflicts." Some instantly responded "no problem," and I would instantly relax. Some simply wanted more explanation. Some I could feel their panic through the phone, some went into some sort of shock. Some yelled at me. One lady cried. But then I realized that somehow in the course of my explanation when I said "not going to make it," she thought I was referring to Yves' life in general, and so she thought I was calling to tell her Yves had died. By the end of our conversation she was so relieved that I think she had forgotten that I called to cancel. I think she may call back later.

Y

I guess you could call it a lobby. Or an atrium. The thing about desert architecture is that it can confuse your understanding of what is "outdoors" and what is "indoors." I enter through the main doors of the H into a large, open room which has several doors, which are actually walls, that open up onto courtyards which may be rooms that have walls that appear to be doors...But I do see right away what looks like a sign-in desk and then next to it a fountain and a table with water and fresh fruit I don't recognize and low slung couches. It's really modern but not cold, minimal and modern-warm, an inviting sort of modern. At the desk I meet a tan, fit man who's got to be at least 70 who welcomes me and asks me my name.

I pause.
I don't know.
I don't know what name to check in under. If word got out I was here, if rumors spread I'd lost my marbles, it could cost me some bookings, and you never know who knows who.

Me: "Uh, Rudy Moody."

Really? I have one chance to come up with a pseudonym, a fake identity for the next period of my life, and I choose "Rudy Moody"? The man looks at me and smiles, nods.

Me: "Everybody calls me Rue. It comes from a family name, Rudicon, but as a kid I went by Rudy until that football movie came out which pretty much ruined it for me so then I changed it to Rue."

Now I'm lying, making crap up just to cover over how embarrassed I am. Maybe this is a nut house. I'm here three minutes and I'm lying and making no sense.

Y

"Well Rue, I'm Bill. Welcome to Hesed House. We're thrilled you're here. Here's your house key, here's a map, you can still catch dinner for another half hour and then you're scheduled to meet Sister at eight at your house."
Me: "Sister?"
Bill: "Her real name is Stasium, but we've called her Sister as long as I can remember. She'll be your guide—she'll help you navigate all that's going on here."
Me: "So is she a shrink or a doctor or what?"
Bill: "She'd laugh if she heard you ask that. Some people might say yes, but no...She's hard to explain. You'll see. Eight at your house."

My "house" is a twelve-by-twelve-foot little stucco hut with a chair, a couch, a bed, a table, a giant window looking out on the valley, and a bathroom. It's clean and sparse and minimal, and it instantly puts me at ease. I don't know if I've ever found a physical space to be so calming. I follow my map to the eating area, which is actually just a bowl carved out of the mountainside, like a giant rock dish, with tables made out of giant slabs of wood and sawed up tree trunks for seats and a buffet. Great food. Lou was right. It's all healthy, lots of olive-oily things—my food vocabulary is a bit limited—and I inhale my dinner. There's only a few other people still eating, and they seem absorbed in conversation so I eat alone. I can't recall the last time I ate alone. What does a person look at when they eat alone? The food? I start off into the distance, taking in the mountain. I keep saying to myself, "Man, that's a big mountain," which I realize is a bit redundant.

R

I hang up the phone with the last of the "yes" calls to EXPLODE applicants. That was quite enjoyable. Calling people and informing them their application has been reviewed and "Yves Green has personally chosen them to join him for this epic weekend of challenge and aspiration." Not a bad gig. Some were quite cool about it, but most were obviously thrilled. When I told one guy he was in, he yelled, "Well, hot damn!" into the phone. I think it's because I added the "Yves has personally chosen" part. It's not true exactly because Claudia and I read the rest of the applications and made decisions without him. But it's true enough. It's true in spirit, whatever that means.

Y

There's a knock at the door of my hut, and I open to find a tiny woman standing there.

"Hello, you must be Rue?
Me: "Hi, yes, I am, I'm...Rue."

"I'm Stasium, but please call me Sister."
Me: "Come on in. I'm sorry—is this where we meet?"

The thought of a second person in the room instantly makes the room seem much smaller and confining. Just trying to invite her in involves moving my duffel bag out of the way and sliding the chair over. Amazing how a space can be perfect for one and unbearable for two.

Sister: "You have two chairs here in front of your house—let's sit there. I find the mountain just about the most perfect thing in the world to look at while you talk about the things that matter most."
Me: "Wow. You don't mess around."
Sister: "No, I don't."

About this time somewhere in the back of my mind I am beginning to collect and organize my first impressions of this woman. She is tiny, did I mention that? I bet ninety pounds soaking wet. She has long, gray hair in a ponytail and a big silver bracelet and a skirt made of what looks like curtains or a tablecloth or something-homemadey if that's a word. But not hippie homemadey, cool homemade, kind of euro or something. And she's got big blue eyes looking straight at me. It's a bit unnerving. And sharp features, distinct.

This is going to sound bizarre, but my first thought when I see her, and it stays with me: "She looks like Mother Teresa." But not in the "feed the poor, that's so special" sort of way, but in an energy, aura, presence sort of way.

She's direct and focused, but it's the coiled up energy within—
there is nuclear power in this woman. And yet she's serene
and calming. I both want to climb the mountain in front of us
with her strength, and I want to sit in front of it and do nothing
all at the same time.

Sister: "So Rue, what brings you to the H?"
Me: "Lots of things, but really just a couple—okay one big
thing. I feel like in my line of work I've come to the end of a
season, like I've gone as far as I can go in that vein, and now I
need to go to a whole new level. And this seemed like a
perfect place to really dig down and figure out what that looks
like..."
Sister: "What is it about your line of work that demands this?"
Me: "Well, you know there's a lot of competition out there, and
if you don't keep raising your game you may fall behind."
Sister: "And so for you, coming here is about improving and
excelling and achieving so that you can win?"
Me: "I don't know if I'd put it that bluntly. I would hope I'm
driven by other things than just winning. I've just always had a
desire to be really, really good at what I do."
Sister: "Rue, can we pause here for a moment?"

What could I say to that? She looks off into the distance and
takes a few deep breaths. By the way, this is something I've
noticed since we started talking: she breathes really slowly
and has no problem pausing before she starts a new sentence

just to get a good breath. I have never noticed someone's breathing before.

And then she turns her hips in her chair so that she's facing me more directly and she says: "Rue, you are paying a thousand dollars a day to be here, correct?"

Me: "Yes, I am."
Her: "That's a lot of money."
Me: "Yes, it is."
Her: So how about you cut out all the bullshit and tell me the truth? Why are you here?"

R

I'm losing the new car smell. Thirteen hundred miles on the car and it's losing it's new smell? Shouldn't there be a guarantee on the car, like a warranty, they could call it the "Odor Promise" or something, maybe not the word "odor," but still, some sort of pledge that this car will hold its new car smell for five thousand miles? And then there could be an asterisk like there always is with new car warranties, that said something like "unless you smoke or have a dog or eat lots of garlic or you already possess uniquely pungent body odor."

Y

I stammer. I stare at the mountain, which has just turned
orange from the setting sun. I try breathing deeply myself.
I look her in the eyes, which are fixed on me with intensity and
what appears to be something else. I think it might be
compassion.

Me: "Sister, I don't know where to begin."
Her: "Let me make a few things clear. We don't rush here, we
take our time. We do this because our assumption is that you
are here for significant, complicated reasons. And those
reasons, whatever they are, have probably unfolded over a
number of years. So to get at them, to unpack them and
understand them, that will take time. Make sense?"
Me: "I think so, I guess I'm just—"

Oh God, this is so embarrassing—am I about to cry? I don't
cry. Other people cry. I make people cry. I watch people cry.
But I don't cry.

Her: "Well, if you've travelled today and gotten settled here
and found your way around that's a solid day. I'll see you
tomorrow. Remember, group is at ten."
Me: "Group?"
Her: "Yes, that's just about the only thing you need to do while
you're here, other than talk with me from time to time, you
need to be at group."

Me: "Group?"

Her: "Yes, I think there are six or seven of you here right now. We'll take turns telling our stories."

Me: "I'm not sure—no offense—if I'm interested in listening to other people tell their stories. I'm here to figure out mine."

Her: "You are, that's true. And there's no better way than group. We're all connected, we're all family."

Me: "You want all the guests to feel connected so we're eating together and telling our stories and all that—sort of like summer camp as a kid?"

Her: "Kind of—but no. I'm not talking about the H. I'm talking about all of us—all of us everywhere. Everybody period."

And with that, she walks out.

R

Another dream last night. Only this time, I had managed to spill new car smell on everything. Somehow I got it on my toothbrush, which gave me new car breath, and I'm at dinner with some woman whose face I can't see because she's holding up her menu, and when I ask the waiter to light the candle at our table it's a scented candle, scented with new car smell, of course. I can't escape it...I'm suffocating in the fumes of my brand newness...

Y

I am staring at myself in the mirror, and it is 9:45 in the morning. I can't decide whether to shave my beard off or not. I have always shaved. Everyday. I now have a beard, and I have gotten through the awful scratchy phase. Between my beard and my stupid fake name, I'm feeling a little dangerous, a little rebellious, a little...foreign. I know who I am, but this guy? The one named Rue in the sweatpants and sandals—who's he?

I don't shave. I am about to put on a t-shirt from an event I spoke at when I catch myself—someone might ask me about it. Why give anybody any information they don't need? I wear something else.

In group we sit in a circle, the seven of us. There's Sister and then next to her is a television and then a large woman in a mumu (what is it about the desert that causes people to go so freestyle in the wardrobe department? Then again, who am I to talk?). And next to her a touristy-looking man in a polo shirt and khaki shorts and he's wearing a fanny pack and then a Middle Eastern-looking gentlemen in his fifties and then me and then a woman in her twenties. She's beautiful, striking, and dressed in something very expensive and current, and then next to her a very plain woman in a white sundress with plain hair who could be 25 or 60. I'm not trying to sound mean — she's just that plain.

We're sitting in plastic chairs, and large windows along one wall of the room open up to the courtyard where we eat. I can see the mountain across the courtyard above the edge of the building. There's a pitcher of water with lemons and a stack of glasses on a small table in the corner and other than that, it's a clean, sparse room, like everything else here.

Sister: "Morning everyone, we have a few friends who came in last night so let's go around and give names."

She then nods and we go around.

Mumu lady: "Brenda".
Fanny pack man: "I'm Steve."
Middle Eastern man: "Faruq." I wonder how you spell that…
Bearded slob in sweatpants—oh yeah, that's me!: "Rue."
Beautiful Young Woman: "Call me Silver."

Yes, that's what she said—her name is Silver. It occurs to me that she must be either rich or famous or both, and Silver is probably her fake name. She reminds me of those pictures in the front pages of those supermarket magazines of celebrities doing normal things in their normal clothes, "And they drink coffee! Just like us!" Only hers would be "They go to expensive health-recovery centers because their lives have totally fallen apart—just like us!"

Plain Lady: "It's Kate."

Sister: "Thank you. I was thinking that this morning, to get the discussion started, I'd play a little video clip, just to help get us talking, give us a sort of starting point...it's only a few minutes but I think you'll enjoy it..."

And then she proceeds to fiddle with knobs and buttons and eventually the screen turns blue and then black and then I see and I hear...

me.

It's a clip from my first video series, years ago. It's a talk I gave around the time that my Bootstraps book came out. I am younger and thinner and I talk very fast and I am very amped up and the crowd is totally into it and I have so much to say and I have this wide-eyed, innocent look in my eyes like someone just handed me the keys to a Ferrari and I can't believe I get to drive it.

It is me. Dear God, it's me.

Did I alienate my family and break an untold number of commitments and travel across the country and out into the desert and lie about my name to pay a thousand dollars a day to listen to myself?

I watch the others, and they are listening intently. Kate has gotten out a notepad and is taking notes. I feel nauseous and terrified and humbled and broken and vulnerable and very, very unsure of myself.

We've been watching me for what feels like a year but has probably only been five minutes when I become aware of rustling beside me. Faruq is shifting his weight in his chair, leaning over to say something to me. He does it discreetly, continuing to face forward so he doesn't distract the others. I smile and lean my head over. He whispers into my ear: "This guy is totally full of shit."

C

I think about Yves often. I wonder how he's doing. Just yesterday Noll and I were at the hardware store, picking up grass seed for a little project in the backyard, when out of nowhere Noll says, "I miss Yves." Noll doesn't say things like that much. Whatever it is Yves needed with this little "time out," I hope he gets it.

Y

A friend of mine was in a car accident in high school in which his mother died but he survived. He told me once that as the car was spinning and flipping and twisting through the air, the thought occurred to him that he knew for sure that his life was never going to be the same again. This is what he was thinking as it was happening. And it's true, the accident and his mother's death changed his life forever. But for many of us, it doesn't work that way. We don't realize until much later that an event or a particular moment was that important. It takes time and hindsight for us to sort through just how significant a particular experience or event will play in our life.

But this moment, sitting here, Faruq's words fresh in my ear, watching myself on the screen, this is one of those moments.

I am spinning and flipping and twisting through the air.

R

I have that dream again, the Ikea one. Only this time I'm being tortured in the back of the store by two employees. They're holding me over a tank filled with a liquid I can't identify, and then they push me under until I think I'm going to die and then they pull me out and yell, "Say it! Say it! Say it!" This happens again and again until I think to ask them—"Say what?"

And they replied:
"It's not a sun roof—it's a moon roof! It's not a sun roof—it's a moon roof!"

So I start shouting, "It's not a sun roof—it's a moon roof!"
over and over again and then I start to smile because it feels
good and I start to sing it. And they start to smile and sing it
with me and stop water-boarding me because they aren't
torturers— they're my friends and don't want to hurt me. They
help me up off the edge of the tank, and they hand me a towel,
which I hold up to my nose after I've dried off because I have
smelled this smell before. They were dunking me in a giant vat
of new car smell...

Y

Sister stops the clip. Faruq looks out the window, Kate puts
her notepad away, Silver twirls her hair. Steve watches Sister.

Brenda: "Can I say something, before we start discussing,
because I know that you're going to invite us to share our
thoughts like yesterday and the day before but I'm so excited I
just can't stand it. That's Yves Green! You played a clip from
Yves Green! What are the odds of that? He's my favorite. And
this one, the Bootstraps challenge 7-part video series—it's
one of my absolute favorites. It's probably not as good as the
Enough with the Sweatpants study guide, but it's good. I have
all of his books and study guides and videos. He is the best. I
can't believe you played a clip from him. Am I talking too
much?"

Sister: "Brenda, your passion and enthusiasm are appreciated by all of us."

She nods to the rest of us, and people nod back and smile and say yes under their breath. I don't do anything. I ought to check myself for a pulse because it doesn't feel like much of anything is happening anywhere in me.

Silver: "I like it, too."
Sister: "What did you like?"
Silver: "Energy. The crowd was totally in to it. Like if you had major problems and you heard him, you might like be inspired and kind of pumped up to do better."
Brenda: "I totally agree. You listen to Yves Green and you feel like you can do anything. Like you could go and climb that mountain right there."
Faruq: "But you can climb that mountain—I did it yesterday."
Sister: "I think Brenda was speaking metaphorically, the mountain being a symbol of something challenging or great, right Brenda?"
Brenda looks confused and others smile awkwardly.
Sister: "And you, Rue, any thoughts?"
Me: "I don't know...I'll have to process it some more..."
Kate: "Me, too. I don't get it."
Sister: "What parts?"
Kate: "All of them, the whole thing. I feel like he's describing a world that doesn't exist. Like the part about 'setting your

course' and 'plotting your path' and keeping your 'compass handy.' What happens when your compass breaks? What happens when you take a turn because the map tells you to and instead of more path, there's cliff? That's why I'm here, because my life is different from the version he's talking about."

The room's energy level has shifted. Everybody is engaged, leaning forward, listening. Steve has lost his deer in the headlights look.

Sister: "Kate, would you be willing to tell us a bit of your story, a bit more on why you're here?"
Kate: "Are you serious? My story? I'm pretty sure I'll bore you all to tears…"
Silver: "No, go for it—we're all ears."
Kate: "Well, okay. Born and raised in Massachusetts, one brother, and my parents are both college professors.
We studied and we achieved in our house, that's what we did. Both of my parents were constantly delivering papers and publishing things and doing research. My brother was a music prodigy—cello and piano and summer camps and private lessons and concerts and Julliard—he's always been the best."

She paused to catch her breath and see if we were paying attention. And we were.

Kate continued: "I was all about science from early on. Experiments and math and projects. So I ended up taking classes at MIT while still in high school, which led to graduate work in astrophysics, which then took me into a Ph.D. in string theory and quantum cosmology which probably sounds like gibberish to you but to me it's…well, my music. At least it was. Getting my degree led to being a professor and doing research and delivering papers all around the world— sound familiar?"

It was clearly a rhetorical question, but Silver said, "Like your parents?"

And Kate nodded before continuing:
"Along the way I met a fellow professor and we fell in love, got married, and now have four kids. We've raised them together and as far as all that goes, I don't think I could have a more perfect life. Which probably has you all wondering why I'm here. About ten years ago I started having problems getting up in the morning. I used to get up at 5 to get some work in before the kids were up.

But then it was 5:30 and it got harder and harder to get up before 6 and then it was 7-And when I would finally get up, sometimes at 8 or 9, I would just feel so heavy, so deflated. By 1 or 2 I would need a nap, which would last a couple of hours. All I wanted to do was go upstairs, close the door to our room, shut the blinds and sleep. My husband eventually took me to a psychiatrist who diagnosed it as 'depression.' Which made sense medically, but me—depressed? What reason would I have to be depressed?"

And so I went on Xanax, but it didn't really help so I ended up going to a different doctor who gave me several different medications and when that didn't work she said that it would take a while, because she was going to have to make subtle adjustments to the cocktail of meds I was taking. By that point, my kids were making their own breakfast and getting themselves off to school, and my husband was doing most of the laundry and groceries. And I…well, I just kept drifting…"

Faruq: "Have you tried anything else?"
Sister: "Faruq, this may not be the best time to ask questions…"
Kate: "No, he's fine—yes, I have tried other things: I've tried running every day, and walking, weight lifting, and strength conditioning. I've tried a protein-only diet, a no-protein diet, lo-carbs, no-carbs, all-carbs. I've sat every morning in front of a blue light, I've used healing oils, I've gone to recovery groups, I've taken Xanax, Zoloft, Prozac, Exlax, Cocaine, Meth, Pot, Brussel sprouts, tai chai, tai kwan do, Red Bull, Mountain Dew, coffee, No Doze—I've tried all of them mixed together in the same glass with a raw egg!"

She was on a roll now. It was unnerving to see her come alive.

"Have I tried anything else, you ask? I've done retreats, seminars, classes, I've been hypnotized, analyzed, I've worked 100 hours a week, I've taken a month of vacation, I've travelled to eight different countries, I've slept with the lights on, lights off, outdoors, in a tent, on the couch, in the basement. I've been to inspirational events, healing services, revivals for religions I don't even believe in, faith healers, snake handlers, I even waited in line six hours in the rain to have the Dalai Lama bless me just to see if that would help. I've painted every room in our house every color imaginable, I have spent thousands of dollars and hundreds of hours and exhausted the patience and perseverance of everybody I know and love to try and get this black dog to leave and in the end, all I want to do, almost every moment of the day is go back upstairs, close the door, shut the blinds, and go to sleep. Does that answer your question, Faruq?"

Faruq is quiet.
If I was Faruq, I would be quiet, too.

Brenda: "You have a black dog? What's its name? I love dogs."
Kate, shaking her head: "Depression …is a black dog. At least that's what we call it. My husband actually got me a puppy for Christmas last year. He was hoping that something "happy

and furry" would lift my spirits. Turns out I'm allergic to dogs, so we had to give it away. My kids cried for a week. Which, as you can imagine, didn't do much for my spirits…"

"Thanks for sharing, Kate."

I realize that it was me who said that. And I meant it. I'm just a bit surprised to hear myself contributing. Weak people "share" in group discussions, not Yves Green. Losers "express" their feelings and "practice vulnerability" with each other. Not winners. Not conquerors. I am having a very difficult time reconciling who I'm supposed to be with how deeply meaningful it was to hear Kate's story. Not to mention how hard it is to reconcile my first impression of Kate with this woman who has just told this story.

She appeared so plain and boring, but she's smart and sharp and quick and brutally honest and she may be depressed, but she's so fierce with reality.

Silver: "That was really deep what you just said, Kate, like so deep, and I respect that. But you haven't really told us why you're here."
Kate: "You're right, I didn't."

She smiles at this. It's like pure light, her smile. "This past summer my oldest daughter worked at a local camp during the days and then at night, she started a screen printing business in our garage, making t-shirts for her friends. Often she'd work late into the night and then get up early and go back to work at the camp. My son got a job with a landscaping company and worked weekends as well as late shifts at a restaurant near our house and my younger daughter taught herself how to sew and then went door to door around our neighborhood, asking people if they had any clothes that needed mending...which unexpectedly got her a ton of work. So they worked and worked and worked, which I didn't think anything of until the first day of school in September when they asked me to have breakfast with them. So I dragged myself out of bed at the ungodly early hour of 8 and went downstairs, and there was a giant sign over the table that said "We love you mom." On my plate at the table was an envelope, and inside it a plane ticket to Phoenix, a map to this place, and all the money they'd made from the summer. They told me they love me too much to ever give up hope that someday, somewhere I'll get the help I need to get better. As my daughter said, "...Because you only get one mom!"

Faruq hangs his head, and there's a tear in his eye.
Brenda is a blubbering mess, wiping her eyes on the corner of her mumu, muttering "That is just the most beautiful thing I have ever heard in my entire life." Silver is biting her lip, trying to act cool, but she can't so she puts her arm on Kate's

shoulder and stares at the floor. Steve is Steve, expressionless.

And Sister? She just sits there smiling, as if this is exactly how she planned it.

She says, "Thank you everybody, and thank you Kate. Next group in two days, here, at 10. Be well." And with that, she walks out of the room.

Y
Khloe: "Hello?"
Me: "Hey babe."
Khloe: "You called—I thought they took away your cell while you're there."
Me: "They did. And they only have one phone here, and it's in this little booth part way up the mountain. I am literally standing in a phone booth next to a giant cactus looking out on a valley, and I can't see one man-made thing."
Khloe: "Sounds like a change of scenery."
Me: "Got that right."
Neither of us know what to say.
Me: "Khloe, is this weird?
Khloe: "Yes, it is. There's a part of me that wants to hear every single detail of what you're doing and seeing and learning and

all that. But there's another part of me that doesn't. Maybe we shouldn't talk for a while?"

Me: "Just share silence on the phone? That's an odd way to rack up a bill."

Khloe: "No, you know what I mean—while you're there. Yves, this is something you need to do and you need to do it all the way. Don't hold anything back. Figure it out. And then, we'll talk—really talk. It'll free you up."

Me: "You sure? Will you be okay? What about Charis?"

Khloe: "We're fine. And then you won't have to climb up any mountains to stand in a phone booth."

Me: "Funny. Ha ha."

Khloe: "I'm hilarious, I know. Go. Do your thing. I love you."

Me: "Yes, I love you. Tell Charis how much I love her, too. We'll talk later."

I walk down the mountain, heavy. But good heavy. Serious heavy.

Making progress heavy.

R

I am on a Volkswagen website, but it's not the official VW site. It's one of the hundreds I've discovered by VW geeks all around the world who obsess over every last detail of their cars. This one is one of the GTI-specific sites, and there are many, with names like "gettinghighinmyGTI.com" and "GTIamonfire.com."

You get the idea. Lots of people with lots of time on their hands. I got here innocently enough. I just wanted to know if I could buy seat covers, maybe leather or with a pattern or something, but I discovered that every single possible thing you could think to add to your car or modify it with has already been invented and is for sale on one of these sites. I have been completely sucked in to this vortex when I come across a guy in Switzerland who specializes in custom VW tattoos, promising that he can give you a tattoo that perfectly matches the exact VW that you drive. I am tempted to send an email to his site asking "What happens if I get in an accident and have to get a new car?" At this point I realize that I have a far more important question: When is Yves going to return so I can get back to work?

Y

I spend the rest of the day staring at the mountain. Hours pass and I do nothing but stare and think. My thoughts follow no continuous stream, bouncing around wherever they like: childhood, Dallas, college, Khloe, moving, tomatoes—it makes no sense to me what my mind is pulling up and it doesn't matter. It is inexplicably perfect to stare at that mountain without a single care. Sister stops me at dinner to ask if I'd like to take a walk in the morning. I almost blurt out, "I would love that!" because that's what I'm thinking, but I casually reply "See you then." Because Rue is one cool cat.

C

When we're home eating together at our table, Noll has this little mock prayer ritual he does when he first sits down. He looks up and folds his hands dramatically and says, "I am deeply convinced that you do not exist but if you do, thanks for the meal," and then he eats. Tonight, he looks up and says, "I am more convinced than ever that you are a myth, invented to keep the masses in fear and submission, but in the slim chance that you do actually exist, I ask that you put your arm around my friend Yves wherever he is tonight."

Y

I am gasping for breath, and we are barely around the base of the small hill next to the big mountain. I am made all the more aware of my pathetic shape by the simple fact that Sister isn't even sweating.

She stops to wait for me, and then says, "So how was group for you?

Me: "Group? It was awesome. But it left me with lots of questions."

Sister: "Fire away."

Me: "It didn't resolve."

Sister: "That's a question?"

Me: "You just let them sit there. Like when Kate was done. You just smiled and then left."

Sister: "What should I have done?"

Me: "How come you didn't say anything? Or draw any conclusions? Or make some wise statement that we could all benefit from? Or give her some practical steps to get better."

Sister: "Like, 'Kate, your children obviously love you so much. It's so touching to see something so beautiful in the midst of the darkness you've been experiencing.' Something like that?"

Me: "Come on, now you're mocking me. That's totally lame."

Sister: "Lame?"

Me: "Yes, lame. Cheap. Weak. Pathetic. Depression is awful—debilitating. Every time she talked about wanting to go back to bed, I felt the heaviness. I felt it in her, I felt in the room, I felt it in me."

Sister: "Exactly. So if you understand depression so well, why didn't you make some wise statement or give her some steps?"

Me: "I can't."

Sister: "And what makes you think I can?"

Me: "Well, at least explain it for us…"

Sister: "Explain what? Explain why this good, loyal, loving, brilliant woman who has selflessly given herself to her family and work has some sort of chemical or psychiatric or genetic or spiritual aberration that has made her want to climb back in bed every moment of every day? Explain it? It can't be explained. Can you imagine anything more offensive than to explain it?

We walk in silence for a hundred yards or so. We come to a flat rock that juts out over a ravine.

Sister: "Let's sit for moment—it appears you need it."

We dangle our feet over the edge. A gecko or lizard or something like that runs by. We don't have those in Ohio.

Sister: "Here's my point, Rue. Some things can't be conquered. Some things just are. What Kate has been told again and again is that she just needs to find the will to conquer it. Like every problem has an answer if you're just willing to throw yourself in to it long and hard enough."

Me: "To Faruq's question. When he interrupted her, part way through her story. The first thing he did was essentially ask her if she'd done everything she could. Which led her to that long rant about all the remedies she's tried."
Sister: "That was something, wasn't it?"

Me: "Oh man, it was stunning. It was like a performance piece or a spoken word rant or something. I was exhausted by the end."

Sister: "And that was her point. I guarantee that her list was only scratching the surface. I bet she's tried such exotic and costly and strange things to get healed that she doesn't even mention them to most people for fear of what they'll think."

Me: "But when you're desperate and you're living in that much agony..."

Sister: "You'll try anything."

Me: "Yes, you will."

Sister: "So what was your point about Faruq's question?"

Me: "What he was really doing was pressing her to find out how hard she'd tried to get better, as if the answer was effort. That was my first thought listening to her, I thought to myself, 'Well, there must be a doctor or treatment or book or something she simply hasn't discovered yet.' Which is essentially saying 'if she would just try harder.' That's probably why she reacted with that fiery list. She's probably had well meaning people suggest all sorts of things for years. Either explicitly or implicitly letting her know that they think she just needs to do more."

Sister: "But some things—"

Me: "—some things don't work that way. You come to the end of your will or strength or whatever you want to call it, and it's not better. It's exactly how it is."

Sister: "And those things—"

Me: "—those things can't be conquered. And until you're in
that spot, up against one of them, you just don't get it.
You have no idea what's it like."

For the first time, I notice that Sister is wearing a "Virginia Is for
Lovers" shirt and that her hiking boots look really worn. Like
she's walked in them for thousands of miles.

We walk some more, around another little hill, down through a
ravine, across a river bed, and when we make it back, she
says as we part, "Dwight will stop by before dinner—make
sure you're in your house."

Dwight? This place is an alternate reality. I'm used to
schedules and plans and knowing who is going where and
how things are going to unfold. But here, at the H, all I get is
that "Dwight" will be stopping by. Whoever Dwight is…

K

I saw a friend today at the market, and she asked, "So what
part of the world is Yves in today?" and then she laughed. It's
a bit of a joke with some of my friends, the fact that my
husband has this exotic, traveling life. He sounds so
glamorous to them, coming and going and reading fan mail
when he's home. I consider for a moment answering her:
"Well, the last I saw him he was wearing sweatpants and

sandals, and he had a beard and a gut and was going to the desert to find himself."

Y

I stop by the front desk after our walk. Bill is there.

Me: "Hi, Bill, could I bother you for some paper and pen?"
Bill: "Sure, I've got it right here."
Me: "Perfect, thanks."
Bill: "How's it going?"
Me: "It's going great. I am sleeping like I haven't slept for years. I mean ten, eleven hours with no problem. It's like some sort of magic bed or something."
Bill: "It's all about the thread count, I like to say."
Me: "Thread count?"
Bill: "Yes, the density of a fabric is measured by how tightly the threads are woven together, the higher the thread count, the higher the quality."
Me: "Right. And let me guess—the sheets here have a high thread count?"

Bill just smiles. So I lean my elbow on the counter, and tilt my head forward, like Bill and I are sharing top secret, scandalous information. I lower my voice, "I'm so glad you said that. Because I knew there had to be something different about this bed, but I couldn't figure out what it is. And I thought about coming out here and asking you or whoever was working, but I thought that might be a little odd. But this explains it. This little thread-count detail makes a huge difference."

Bill: "Of course it does. You've just articulated one of our core philosophies."
Me: "You have philosophies about thread count?"
Bill: "You could put it that way. Let me ask you a question: Do you know anybody with an empty closet?"
Me: "No, everybody complains that theirs are full and overflowing."
Bill: "And when people are buying a house, one of the things they're looking for—"
Me: "—one of the things they're looking is how many closets it has."
Bill: "But you and I both know that all that stuff is just that—stuff. It doesn't make your life any better. It often gets in the way. I remember being in Rome a while ago, and my wife and I were wandering around the streets behind the Sistine Chapel when we came to this little neighborhood bistro, maybe four or five tables. The owner seated us and poured us each a glass of wine, and the table had a simple white tablecloth on it. Then he brought out this perfect loaf of bread, and he placed a plate between us filled with the best olive oil I've ever tasted. I ordered pasta, I believe it was tagliatelle, with a pesto sauce. It came out on a big, white plate. It was the perfect portion of pasta and sauce, all alone on a big clean perfect white plate. It

was just so simple. So pure. And so good. Just a few ingredients, olives and grapes and grain, and yet done with so much care and attention to quality. The Italians figured this out with food, but with clothes as well. Ever notice their men's suits? They're rarely bulky or cluttered—just a perfectly chosen fabric with a clean, crisp, trim cut and excellent craftsmanship. So much less and yet so much more."

I look at Bill and wonder what else I don't know about him. We're having a conversation about thread count and pasta and the cut of men's suits in Italy and I am enjoying it.

Me: "And this is why you have water in every room in the place, water with lemons, and you don't have a pop machine?"
Bill: "Oh, can you imagine? A soda machine with cans and a bright light and plugged into the wall with that electric hum going all the time, just so we can fill ourselves with high fructose corn syrup, surely the most heinous substance in the American diet."
Me: "Too much clutter?"
Bill: "Too much clutter."
Me: "Is this why my room is so calming?"
Bill: "Of course. Take a great, clean, white space and only put in it the essentials. Think through every last detail. Remove all clutter. We thought about putting end tables on either sides of the bed, but someone asked 'Why?' and someone else

answered 'Because that's what they put in hotels.' But this isn't a hotel and 'we' aren't 'them.' Never make assumptions because it works for someone else. What works for this place in this time with what we're doing here? That's the question."
Me: "The world is too cluttered."
Bill: "Yes it is, Rue."
Me: "We eat whatever and we look at whatever and we wear whatever and we fill rooms with things because that's how we've seen it done, not because it's the most intentional, precise to do."
Bill: "Well said, that could be a speech or something!"
Me: "It probably could."

Does he know who I am and what I do? I begin to walk away but I turn around. One last question: "Bill, do you own this place?"

He smiles. "Let's just say I have a vested interest in all of this doing well."
Me: "Anyway, thanks for the paper. And the lecture on Italian aesthetics."

I take my paper back to my guesthouse because Sister has stirred up so much for me, and she drops so much brilliance on me, that I have to write it down. But somehow the words don't do it justice.

"Some things just are."

I stare at it and I read it out loud. I am frustrated because there are layers of meaning and depth to those words. It's just that I can't describe what that is right now. I can't remember the context in which Sister said it, all of the things she said before and after it. Maddening.

"Some things just are."

Imagine if my competition saw me now, hunched over this table in a hut in the desert repeating a meaningless phrase to myself again and again, as if by sheer force of will I could conjure some sort of meaning out of it. They would shake their heads, saying to those around them, "If you could have seen him in his prime..."

I hear a knock, open the door, and there before me stands a man in his mid-to-late sixties, tall, stooped over, with a white beard and a bald head with hair on the sides. A green t-shirt, tweed sport coat, and hiking pants round out his "outfit." He and Sister probably shop together.

"Hello, I'm Dwight."
Me: "Yes, yes, Dwight—Sister said you'd stop by."
Dwight: "I thought I'd drop something off before we meet the day after tomorrow."

Me: "We have a meeting the day after tomorrow?"

Dwight: "Did Sister not tell you? How many times have I let her know that not all of us thrive on the unknown, just floating along, pretending like we're making this up as we go along? I'm always the one reminding people that we take ourselves seriously here and that there should be at least some resemblance to a professional institution of health and counseling."

I immediately like Dwight. A lot. A man after my own heart.

"Anyway, I'll be one of your guides here. I'm a licensed psychologist, Ph.D. and all that, blah blah blah. I've been doing this for thirty years and I love it. The first thing I'd like to do is discuss this book with you."

I notice as he hands me the book that his hands are gnarled, like he has arthritis or something.

I take the book.

"I wanted to give it to you personally. If you had been handed this book and told that you should read it because somebody you've never met thinks you should, you would probably do what I would do and toss it. But if I hand it to you and tell you that I'm looking forward to discussing the prologue with you the day after tomorrow at one, well, that changes things, doesn't it?"

Me: "Yes, it does."

Him: "Good. But enough of my chatter, the day after tomorrow, one o'clock, I'll see you at my rock. Peace."

And with that, he's gone. What is it with these people and their exits?

Although it does work. I take the book and examine it. It's thin, which is good. I can't stand long books where the person goes on and on to try and say something they could have in a couple of words. The author's name is Abraham Joshua Heschel.

The title of the book is The Sabbath.

Sabbath? Isn't that a Jewish thing? Did Dwight give me a religious book? Because that's not gonna fly. If this place has some sort of secret religious agenda, I will leave right now, even if it means I have to climb over that mountain on my hands and knees to do it. I did not come here to find God.

R

I don't have any dreams tonight, which is nice. A nice break from things at Ikea falling on me and people water boarding me with smells from which I cannot escape. How pathetic is it when not having strange dreams is nice?

Y

I sleep ten and a half hours. For a split second I'm embarrassed that I've managed to sleep this late into the morning, but my embarrassment is cut short because I look around the room, and I am reminded that it takes at least two for there to be embarrassment. And I am alone. And it is 9 and group is in an hour. And I can't wait for group. Four days here and I'm looking forward to going to a group therapy meeting. I clearly remember mocking people who go to group therapy. I used to make jokes about people who have to go to meetings all the time just to get through the day. It just seemed so...so...weak to me. Just change your habits. It's really quite simple. Right?

The same people are at group, and we sit in the same chairs. Silver is wearing a white linen princess-in-the-desert sort of number, and Steve is still rockin' the fanny pack. Brenda has managed to wear a mumu that reminds me even more of a circus tent, and Kate is plain Kate, and, after some opening hello's, Faruq says he'd like to tell his story:

"I grew up in Tehran, the north part, the part with money. My father owned an electronics store. We weren't rich— my father sold televisions and appliances to the rich, but in the seventies there was such a black cloud over our lives not knowing where Iran was headed. And when my father saw the revolution taking shape, he told me that if I didn't leave now, I'd never be able to. And so he paid for me and my brother and sister to be smuggled out of the country, a big business back then involving secret handshakes and envelopes full of cash. He paid what the equivalent of about $45,000 would be, fifteen for each of us. We waited at the place we were told, and at just the right time in the night, a truck picked us up. They laid us in a row under the floorboards in the back and we rode for hours like that until we got to the border. There was a moment when the guards were at their farthest distance apart on their patrol when you made a run for it. It's treacherous because all the money, preparation, and secrecy means nothing if crossing that little stretch of sand doesn't go right for you."

Faruq paused to drink from a glass of ice water. He continued:

"Finally, they gave us the signal and we jumped out of the truck and ran. It was terrifying—so cold and so dark, and the sand was so deep, way deeper than they said it was. We were running for our lives and could see the border, and my brother starts to lag behind and I called to him, 'Saiid, Saiid— you must keep going.' But he's losing his breath, and while I'm running slower to stay with him, our sister Hosne was getting farther and farther ahead. Then I got mad at him and told him, 'This is the wrong time to lag behind!' But he doesn't acknowledge my urgency so I say it louder, and I say his name, demanding him to run faster. When still he moves so slowly, I yell louder—then realize too late my mistake. The guards hear me and start running toward us. They have chased people like us many times, and so now I'm shouting at my brother, tugging on his arm. I am doing everything I can to get him to see that he's almost there, but he has no wind in him, no strength. And then I hear our sister yelling, "Don't forget me Faruq! Come on!" She was getting close to the other side, and I realized I had to choose between my brother and my sister.

I was torn but for only a moment because my sister had not stopped repeating, "Don't forget me Faruq! Don't forget me Faruq!" And so I let go of my brother, and I ran towards her and the guards began to close in. They were shouting but I could hear only the sound of my own heart throbbing in my ears as I ran to join my sister. Then I heard them yell, "Stop running or we'll shoot!" Then I heard the sound of gunfire as I crossed the border and embraced my sister. And then I turned around to see my brother lying face down in the sand, which was the last time I ever saw him."

Faruq pauses and stares at the floor.
Faruq is still, and it feels like every one of us has stopped breathing. Then after an interminable silence, he goes on:

"And so my sister and I made our way to America, where I determined to make my brother's death and my father's sacrifice mean something. I worked and worked and worked. I started at minimum wage working for ABC Warehouse because it was the first electronics store in the phone book—which is a big deal when you're learning English—and soon I was managing several of them, and then owning them, and then buying other stores and businesses. I became a very wealthy man with a wife and children—but they barely know me. Somehow I got it all wrong. And that's why I'm here."

Faruq sighed deeply, and I began to breathe again.

Sister: "Thank you Faruq, I was hoping—"
Faruq: "Actually, that's not the specific reason why I'm here. My sister phoned me several weeks ago to tell me the news: my son and his wife just had a baby boy. Obviously, it was painful to hear this news from my sister and not from them—from him, my son. But do you know what broke my shattered heart? She told me that when she asked him if he'd called me to tell me the news, you know what he said to her, he asked her, "Why would I do that?"

I'm sitting there and I feel for Faruq. I ache for Faruq. I hurt for Faruq. I can't begin to imagine that this man sitting next to me is carrying that kind of pain around with him. How does he even get up in the morning?

Faruq keeps going:

"And that's why I have such a problem with what that guy was saying in the video we watched a couple of days ago. I did what he was saying to do in the video. I picked myself up by my bootstraps. I did exactly what he says to do. I worked harder and longer and I let nothing stand in my way and nothing discourage me and I refused to be a victim and I resisted the urge to blame my tragedy on anybody. Yes, I did what he said and in the end, look where it's gotten me: I'm rich but old and tired—and alone."

R

I'm sitting on my couch (yes, I got it from Ikea, but it was a while ago, like two years or something before it got popular to get your furniture there), and I'm going through the names of my friends on my phone: Rick? Nope, he's busy with his family. Bernie? He's got a date tonight. Yes, Bernie has a date, and I'm home alone? That is cosmic injustice. Will? Out of town on business. Dane? Studying for the bar exam. Juan? Annoying me lately, really getting on my nerves.

What's that about? I can't find anybody to call? I scroll through more names, but they all seem so stale—not the people so much as the friendships. We have an informal routine: I'm in town a couple of times a month, and we go out and get dinner, a few beers, see a movie, catch a game, go for a run, hit a party, whatever—and then I leave for a while. My friends are twice-a-month friends. Last time I was in we went out for dinner for Will's birthday—after about an hour, the evening lost its steam. We didn't have anything more to talk about. We covered work, high school friends we'd seen, sports (the Cavs mostly—definitely not the Bengals or Browns), women, cars, and then we were done! The next hour or so was mindless chat. And so I sit here on my couch scrolling back and forth, from the A's to the Z's, from the Z's back through to the A's...no one.

Y

Faruq: "I played by the bootstraps rules only to find out that they're the rules for a different game, a game I don't want to be playing anymore. I don't care anymore whether or not I'm winning—it's the wrong game. I've won the wrong game and lost the right game."
Kate: "I was thinking last night that the bootstraps thing doesn't really work for me, either. Not for the same reason as Faruq—by the way, thank you for sharing. I was very moved. But the bootstraps idea, what about when you can't?"
Sister: "When you can't what?"
Kate: "When you can't conquer something. I'm not convinced life works that way—not everybody can just throw themselves into something and "give it all you got" and "just do it" and all that—"

Steve: "That's a good point."

Yep, he still had his fanny pack. I wonder what's in it.

Sister: "Would you like to say more, Steve?"

Steve: "No. Not really."

Kate seems to be getting increasingly animated. And I'm also noticing, and this might sound a little odd, that the plainness seems to vanish when she's talking. And she's talking right now: "…and it's like when I get up in the morning. I've tried everything to 'put a positive spin on things' and I've 'counted my blessings' and every other cliché, and yet some mornings I want to kill myself."

Silver: "Totally." The way she says it makes me think there is more behind it. She returns to examining her nails.

Brenda: "That's why I think Yves is so inspiring."

Faruq: "Who's Yves?"

Brenda: "The speaker in the video."

Faruq: "Bootstraps man?"

Brenda: "Yes, that's why he's so inspiring—I hear him and I just know every thing's going to be okay."

Kate: "How do you know this?"

Brenda: "Oh, it's just a feeling I get."

Kate: "But what if that feeling is wrong? What if it's not going to be okay? What if it doesn't matter what we do or don't do?"

Brenda: "Well, I think you have to learn to trust your feelings."

Kate: "But my feelings tell me on a regular basis to take one of my husband's belts and loop it around the clothes pole in our closet and hang myself."

Me: "I don't think 'trusting your feelings' is his point in the video. I don't think his goal is that people will have a certain good feeling. It takes way more than that to get ahead or succeed or sometimes even to survive."

I can't believe I'm trying to help someone understand what I really meant in a video I made over a decade ago. But I'm Rue, not Yves, right? They don't know it's me.

Kate: "What is his point, then?"
Me: "He's trying to get people to take action."
Kate: "But what if you can't? Or what if you do take action and it doesn't change anything?"
Faruq: "I think the guy has got it wrong on both accounts—Brenda said it helps her just to feel good but that's only a feeling, and we all know that won't get you much farther than the moment you're in. Or you do what he says and you take action only to discover that it was the wrong action and you find out too late that life is about more than winning."

Brenda: "It's very personal to me, what his talks mean to me. They pick me up just when I need it."
Me: "Really? What do you need it for? Did anything you've ever heard him say or anything you've ever read in any of his books ever actually cause you to change your life?"
Brenda: "Of course. He helps me forget my problems and focus on the positive."

Me: "And what are those? What are your problems? How has Yves Green ever helped you change or overcome anything?"

Uh-oh. Not good. That came out wrong. Too much edge. A bit accusatory. She's about to burst.

Brenda leans forward in her chair, her face turning red, and glares at me: "What is your problem with Yves Green?"

K

I awoke this morning and sat up in our bed, alone. Which is how I wake up most mornings of my life. Usually when I wake up, and he's on the road, I may think about Yves for a moment or two, but I can always picture him in a hotel room some-where, going over his notes for his talks, ironing a shirt, eating breakfast in the restaurant in the lobby. Even if I don't know exactly where he is, and I don't even try to keep track anymore, I can still picture your average room in your average hotel in your average city somewhere. But this morning I can't do that. I can't find the mental picture—there's no visual, just an empty space. An empty space in my mind and an empty space in the bed.

Y

Me: "I'm sorry Brenda—do I sound like I have a problem with Yves Green? Please forgive me. I'm sure he's a good man, but I think he lives in a world that is a lot less complex than the world we all actually live in. He's just too cut and dried and too confident for where I live."

Brenda: "Well, I think you should listen to more of his videos or maybe read one his books before you judge him like that."

Sister: "Thank you, Brenda, that's an excellent suggestion, and thank you, Rue, for reaching out to make amends with Brenda."

Me: "I was thinking, if I may Brenda, could you tell us a bit about why you're here and where you're coming from?"

Head nods from the group to encourage this direction. Brenda smiles as she becomes aware of just what it would mean to be the unquestioned center of attention. She says, "Remember 'Unbranded'?"

Kate: "Unbranded?"

Brenda: "Yes, in the grocery story, in the late eighties. Remember that brand that was called 'Unbranded' with the black and white packaging?"

Faruq: "They made things that looked and tasted almost exactly like popular brands but much cheaper, right?."

Brenda: "That was my parents' company. When I was a kid,

one night we were eating waffles or cupcakes or something like, and my mom started to read the ingredients. 'I could make these,' she said and got out the ingredients and did it. My dad took a bite and said, 'I could sell these. My dad was always complaining about the advertising on television and the way we get bombarded by branding and advertising when, as he put it, 'it's all the same crap anyway.' And so my mom copied the recipes and my dad sold the brand and they started hiring employees, and they bought one warehouse and then another..."

Silver: "I've never seen any brand called 'Unbranded' in any store."
Brenda: "Correct—you haven't. They sold it after six years and made a hundred million dollars."
Silver: "But that doesn't explain why I've never seen it."
Brenda: "The people who bought it decided to brand it—you know, 'the unbrand'—so they trademarked it and hired a marketing company and made commercials and—"
Faruq: "—and they killed it."
Brenda: "Exactly."
Faruq: "Classic error. They mistook their market share for consumer loyalty and in the process created unnecessary dissonance in the mind of the buyer about the essence of their product's identity...what a shame."
Sister: "But Brenda, how does that lead to your being here?"

Brenda: "Right. When I turned twenty, I received my share of the money. Which means I've been able to do whatever I want and go wherever I want and buy whatever I want for the last nine years."

Silver: "Sounds great—what's the problem?"

Brenda: "It was. No problem until earlier this year, when my parents showed up unexpectedly at the villa I was renting in Ibiza to take me to dinner and tell me that if I didn't do something with my life, I would lose the money. I told them I'm an adult, and I can do what I want with my life—it's my money. They then informed me there's a clause in the trust that gives them the power to revoke my share up until I'm thirty years old for any reason 'at their discretion as they see fit.'"

Silver: "That's tough."

Brenda: "So that's what I've been doing here, sorting out what I'm going to do with my future. Dwight said in one of our sessions that I suffer from the 'inertia of options.' I didn't understand what he was saying at the time, but as I've had time to reflect on it, it made sense. Because I can do whatever I want, I have all of these options. And all of these options make it hard to actually pick one."

Kate: "It's called the 'slavery of freedom.'"

Brenda: "It is?"

Kate: "It's possible to have so much freedom that a person becomes paralyzed, unable to decide on a course of action. Limits can be a gift. Can I ask you a question?"

Brenda: "Sure…"

Kate: "What exactly have you done for the past nine years?"
Brenda: "Well, I was in Paris for a while, but that city is just so dirty and overrated so I decided to move Milan and apprentice with a famous fashion photographer. But the hours were unbearable—that man was a slave driver! After that I decided to live among the poor, but two weeks in India and I was ready to face the fact that helping the poor, well, it's just not my thing. Then I enrolled in a business program at the University of..."

And then it happens. I watch it happen. Everybody does. What I watch happen I can't describe adequately with words other than to say that the lights came on. Brenda was in the middle of her speech, and she's reciting all of the places she's lived and things she's tried and then she just stopped talking because in answering Kate's question she ended up telling her story for the past nine years. And in telling her story out loud she had to hear her story, not just think it and experience it.

And as she heard her own story told out loud, she got this look on her face like she was hearing it for the first time. Like she was standing outside of herself, looking in. And then Brenda, who talks every chance she gets and wears on all of our nerves after only two groups, gets quiet. Really quiet.

Brenda: "Well, that's enough about me. Thanks for listening."
And with that, she stops talking.

Sister: "And with that, we're done. Two days from now, same time, same place. Peace."

Group is over. Silver gets something to drink. Steve just sits there. Kate puts her notebook away. Faruq gets up out of his seat and walks over and motions to Brenda to stand, and she does and then he gives her a hug. I walk quickly out of the room, through the courtyard, behind the building, in among some cactus, where I sit down and stare at the mountain for the next hour.

R

Should I call Yves? Leave him a message? Write him a letter? Is he checking email? What is he doing? I'm terrified he will decide we're never going back on the road.

Y

I don't know what that was. Something about the way Faruq didn't say anything—he didn't make a show of it, he just hugged her. Something about the simplicity of it, the solidarity of it. So pure. And it was coming from Faruq, who isn't exactly the embodiment of empathy. It was just so moving.

Here it is, a couple of hours later, and I'm still reflecting on it. And not just that image of Faruq hugging her, but what it did to me. It caused all these totally unfamiliar emotions to be unleashed in me. I have lost it. I have become a blubbering mess.

I sit in my chair in front of my little house, and I open the book Dwight gave me. All I have to do is read the Prologue? How hard can that be? Only eight pages...I'll be done in a few minutes, and Dwight will be impressed.

Page one, first line: "Technical civilization is man's conquest of space."

Huh? I thought this was some sort of Jewish book. And here it starts with something about putting a man on the moon.

Next sentence: "It is a triumph frequently achieved by sacrificing an essential ingredient of existence, namely, time." Ingredients? Time? Is this a cooking metaphor? The third sentence of the book: "In technical civilization we expend time to gain space."

I don't get this. I am lost. I consider myself intelligent, but three sentences in and I have no idea what this man is talking about. "Gain space?" Why does he keep talking about space? Is this science fiction? What kind of story is this supposed to be?

At least my books have a point. It's very clear and I include diagrams and bullet points. I want people to sit down with one of my books, open to the first page, and get something out of it right away. Life is way too short, and we're all way too busy, and there is way too much to get done to read difficult books written by authors who haven't done the hard work of distilling their thoughts into a few simple lines everybody can understand.

I keep reading and I come across this line: "To enhance our power in the world of space is our main objective."

What is this—a brochure for NASA? Remember Haikus, those Asian poems that contain only so many syllables in three short lines and capture one image or observation? Heschel sure does: "Yet to have more does not mean to be more."

It's like bad Haiku! Or something you'd read in a fortune cookie!

I liked Dwight and he seemed to be somewhat professional, but this book assignment lowers his stock in my eyes. I don't know what Dwight and I are going to talk about when we get together because I'm going to have to be honest with him. This is a terrible book.

K

One of my Big Girl distributors asked me today what my husband is up to—he's a big fan. I told him Yves was away, assuming that would be enough. But it wasn't. This guy wanted to know where he was speaking. So I told him that Yves was in Arizona, assuming that would be enough. But it wasn't. He got really excited and said he has a sister in Arizona and he's been telling her all about Yves and how he works with Yves' wife (Works with? How about works for?). He asked, "Where in Arizona?" I stalled and stared at the ground and said, "Oh, it's in the middle of nowhere." He laughed, "Everywhere in Arizona is the middle of nowhere!" And then he asked the name of the venue. I said, Yves was at a "private event, you know, invitation only, that sort of thing." He said, "But you're his wife, you can't get a ticket for my sister?"

This is not working for me. Not at all.

Y

I remember as I leave my house that I have no idea where to meet Dwight—all he said was his "rock." I ask around and I'm told to take a right at the phone booth. These people are mental. And so I dutifully go up the mountain. I take a right at the phone booth and sure enough, there's a trail I hadn't noticed the first time I was up here.

I follow the trail past the phone booth, around a group of huge rocks, they must be ten feet tall, and there I find Dwight, sitting in a chair, barefoot, reading a book. There's another chair next to his, and between them there's a table with a pitcher of water with lemons in it (surprise, surprise) and a footrest between the chairs. It's like a living room... on the side of a mountain in among cactus and rocks.

Dwight: "Rue, so good to see you—please, sit down."
Me: "This is quite a little set up you have here."
Dwight: "You should see the sunrise from here. It's like you're the only person on the earth when 'the dawn rises up and takes the earth by its edges.' That's a line from one of my favorite poems."
Me (not quite knowing what to say to that): "Well, here we are. I read that book you gave me. At least the part you wanted me to, the Prologue."

I sound like a boy trying to impress his teacher. Dwight has this effect on me despite giving me a terrible book to read. He's so still. It could be the setting, but I think it's also him. He's a perfect match for the setting. By the way, he's wearing old trousers that were cut off above the ankles and a trucker hat and a t-shirt that says "G-RAP" on it.

Dwight: "And what did you think?"

Me: "Well, Heschel is clearly a deep thinker…I felt like he took his time making his points, and I—"
Dwight: "Are you lying, Rue?"
Me: "Yes, I am."

I don't feel bad admitting it. He has the same sort of power that Sister has—they are sharp and smart, and yet you can be totally honest and you don't feel like you're going to be judged for it. So I continue: "I hated it. I didn't get it. It made no sense, and the more I read it, the more lost I got, if that's possible. It might as well have been in another language."

Dwight: "It kind of is."
Me: "Which one?"
Dwight: "Heschel is his own type of other language. And learning new languages takes time."
Me: "I'm not following you."
Dwight: "Let's break it down to its smallest parts. What exactly didn't you get?"
Me: "How about the first line? He starts talking about NASA and stuff and then he totally changes the topic."

Dwight laughs a deep, throaty laugh that would normally cause a person to laugh as well when they heard it. It's that contagious. But I don't laugh because the laugh is clearly at my expense. He then says, "Technical civilization is man's conquest of space."

Me: "Yes, that's it. You have it memorized?"

Dwight: "It's classic."

Me: "What makes it classic?"

Dwight: "He's not talking about NASA here. He's talking about physicality. Earth, the material world. Soil and clothes and money and bodies—he's talking about the world we can access with our senses."

Me: "So he's not talking about outer space?"

Dwight: "No, he's talking about our world."

Me: "Then why doesn't he just say that?"

Dwight: "Because he has a larger point. He opens the book by saying that our modern world, with all of our technology and advancements and factories and innovations has been about conquering what we can see. So in that sense, yes, you could say putting a man on the moon is a part of that. But there is a cost to all of that conquest."

Me: "Which is…?"

Dwight: "Notice the second line…"

He hands me his book because I didn't bring mine. Which humbles me because I'm trashing this book that I don't even have in front of me. Not only did I not understand it, but now I can't even read what I don't get. I am chastened.

I read the line: "It is a triumph frequently achieved by sacrificing an essential ingredient of existence, namely, time."

Dwight: "Make sense?"

Me: "Not really."

Dwight: "Read the next line."

Me: "'In technical civilization we expend time to gain space.'"

Dwight: "He's setting up contrasting objectives. There is stuff, which he later calls 'thingness.'"

Me: "Yes, I remember thinking what a vague word "thingness" is."

Dwight: "Yes, thingness is Heschel's word for stuff, which is the word we use. He's establishing these two things we pursue, the first being thingness. We work and we labor and we stress ourselves to get things. Nine to Five. Forty hours a week. Fifty weeks a year. We work the hours, which is time, to get paid so that we can buy things. We trade the one for the other. We earn a paycheck, we spend it. We buy, we consume, we conquer, we achieve, we win."

Me: "I know all about that."

Dwight: "Apparently you know about that. But what he's saying here is that life isn't just about things. It isn't just about how much we can accomplish and accumulate in a certain amount of time. Time is useful for other things as well."

Me: "Which is why he uses the word sacrifice?"

Dwight: "Yes. He says that it's possible to have worked so hard and pushed yourself so far and put in so many hours that you've accumulated things but you've missed time."

Me: "How do we miss time?"

Dwight: "Let me ask you a question. Do you have any kids?"

Me: "Yes, a daughter."

Dwight: "Tell me about her birth."

I tell him what I remember, including the part where Khloe grabbed the doctor by his shirt and yelled in his face: "Give me the drugs!!!" I talk about holding Charis for the first time, hearing her cry for the first time.

Dwight: "Is that a thing?"
Me: "Is what a thing?"
Dwight: "What you just told me."
Me: "Do you mean is Charis a thing?"
Dwight: "No, she's a person. I'm talking about what you just told me. Is it a thing?"
Me: "No. It's a story."
Dwight: "And what do we call stories from the past?"
Me: "History?"
Dwight: "We call them memories. Moments in time that we carry with us forever. What kind of car were you driving the day she was born? What were you wearing? How much money was in your bank account on that day?"
Me: "I have no idea what I was wearing—I guess I could look at the pictures. And I could probably figure out the car, and I could look up old bank records. But what would be the point?"
Dwight: "Yes, Rue, yes, do you see? What you were wearing and what you were driving and your net worth are irrelevant in light of that memory of her birth, aren't they?"
Me: "It's time vs. things, is that what you're saying?"

Dwight: "That's what Heschel is saying. He's saying that in our modern quest for achievement and wealth and thingness, we're losing our awareness of moments. Notice what he says here—"

He points to a line, and I read: "'The power we attain in the world of space terminates abruptly at the borderline of time. But time is the heart of existence.'"
Me: "And my memory of her birth, that's 'the heart of existence'?"
Dwight: "Yes."

Dwight is on fire now. His eyes leap and his feet tap the ground—he is electric. He quotes:

"'There is a realm of time where the goal is not to have but to be, not to own but to give, not to control but to share, not to subdue but to be in accord.'"

Me: "Where'd you get that?"
Dwight: "It's on the next page!"

We both laugh.

Dwight: "It's not always about how much you can get done, Rue, how much we can accomplish. The truly wealthy are the ones who understand the power of moments."

Me (reading ahead): "'We cannot conquer time through space. We can only master time in time.'"

Dwight: "Oh yes, this part is brilliant. He essentially says that working harder, spending more hours trying to obtain things will not get you a better handle on time. You can't get the one through the other. Time functions completely differently than space."

I read another line, which actually makes some sense to me: "'We must not forget that it is not a thing that lends significance to a moment; it is the moment that lends significance to things.'"

Dwight jumps out of his chair and does a little jig around his living room on the side of the mountain. He is clearly brilliant and well read and insightful, but he also has no shame and is willing to look like a child. He keeps repeating in a sing-songy sort of way, "'It is not a thing that lends significance to a moment; it is the moment that lends significance to things.'" For a moment I wonder if we're in some kind of new Dr. Seuss musical—it all feels surreal.

Dwight: "Don't you see, Rue? It wasn't the car you were driving that day. That was just a car. But that was the car that you drove your baby girl home in...The moment— that moment of driving her home for the first time is what makes that car, that thing, significant. And the shirt you were wearing that day? Who cares! But when you look at those pictures, that's the shirt you were wearing the first time you held your girl. Don't you see, Rue? Don't you see?"

Me: "I think so. I think I do."

Dwight: "The moment is what makes those things matter. Not the other way around. Time, moments, the present, something unfolding right here in our midst, that's where life is."

Rue: "And this is why he uses the word sacrifice? Because it's possible to be conquering the world of 'thingness' but at the same time you have very few memories?"

Dwight: "Yes, yes, yes! Read the line that starts 'Every hour is —'"

Me: "'Every hour is unique and the only one given at the moment, exclusive and endlessly precious.'"

Dwight: "Rue, my good man, it's about being awake for the moments. Learn that, and you will begin to be alive in ways you never imagined. Session done, let's meet in three days shall we? Chapter 1?"

R

I decide to have an Edward Norton movie marathon. I rent every movie he's ever been in, and I begin watching them starting with the earliest one. I observe that he looked a lot younger when he was younger.

Y

Silver crosses her legs. She looks out the window with that
look models give when they look out windows in magazine
ads. Kind of spacey and pouty and cool and impersonal all at
the same time. Sister has just asked her if she'd like to tell her
story and she's thinking about it.

Silver: "Okay, I'll do it. But I don't want any of your opinions. I
have enough people telling me how to live my life."
Sister: "Agreed, everybody? Faruq?"

Does she have Faruq's number or what? She is good. Gentle
and kind and kind of disarming with the post-hippie look, but
strong as steel as well. Today her t-shirt reads: "Eat things
from the Earth, not from factories off the New Jersey turnpike."

Silver: "I am a mistake. My parents had two perfect children, a
boy and a girl, and everything was going according to plan,
and then I came along, ten years after my sister. An 'oops
baby.' It's not like they ever said it, but you can tell those
things when you're a kid. My dad owns a hedge fund firm. He
started it in his late twenties when he had just finished
business school. He and his buddies had this hunch that the
market was about to change, which of course it did—that's my
dad. My mom is from three generations of Halcyons, they're
an east coast family that trace themselves back to people who
signed the Declaration of Independence. Marrying my dad was

201

risky because he wasn't part of her family's social circle, but he was so rich at such a young age that she simply started her own social circle, which is what everything is about for my mom. Who you know, what you're wearing, where you vacation. My brother went into my dad's firm out of business school and my sister became a doctor. They're all perfect and successful and the presidents of everything they join. My brother married a woman just like my sister and my sister married a man just like my brother, and they're all members at the same racquet club and we all vacation together at the same resort in the Caribbean in the winter and the same cottage on Martha's Vineyard in the summer. We're the perfect rich successful family. It's like they chose my path for me years before I was even born. My mom will not stop trying to set me up with her friends' sons, these preppy boring frat boys who brag about their internships while they play beer pong in pink shirts."

Kate laughs at this. Which makes Faruq laugh. Which makes me laugh. Steve doesn't laugh, he fidgets with his fanny pack. Silver doesn't see what's funny, but she smiles, anyway.

"But that's not me. None of it. I don't belong, I don't fit, and I'm tired of all of them trying to jam me into a mold of who they think I'm supposed to be. It all came to a head last semester because it's assumed in my family that after undergrad you go to grad school because otherwise, what would you possibly do with your life? That's their attitude: there's one way to be successful and one way to get there and there's nothing more to discuss. But I don't want to be a doctor or a lawyer or a hedge funder."

Silver chokes up. Kate hands her a tissue.

Sister: "What do you want to be?"
Silver: "That's the painful part—I know exactly what I want to do. Since I was young, I have had a fascination with rooms and buildings and environments. I walk into a room and I just know what to do to it to make it feel better, more alive. For as long as I can remember, I have loved to rearrange furniture and redecorate spaces. When I was eight, my parents sent me to a shrink—at a hundred dollars an hour—because I kept redesigning my bedroom. They thought I was obsessive compulsive or something. And so I went to get "fixed," but I ended up showing the shrink how he had his desk in the wrong spot and needed to orient his chairs around the windows and not the door. He refused to charge my parents because he said he would have had to pay much more to an interior designer to tell him the same thing. And what did my parents do? Sent me to another shrink who said I was ADD and gave me some medication."

Silver looks around at each of us, as if she's trying to decide whether or not to keep going.

"This is what I want to do with my life—study design and help people live in better spaces. Most people have no idea how huge our environments are and what a significant role they play in our happiness. And most spaces are just wrong. Most stores, most restaurants, and don't get me started on houses. During my freshman year, everybody who came into my dorm room was like 'Oh my God, this is the best dorm room I've ever been in—can you do this to mine?' So I started designing my friends' rooms and telling them where to put things and how to arrange them. So they called me the 'Chi Chick' because I used the word 'chi' a lot back then. By the way, that's why this place is so great—have any of you noticed anything about your sleep?"

Me: "Yes! I sleep like a baby here."
Brenda: "Me, too."
Kate: "I do, too, but that's not unusual."
Silver: "Of course—the people who built this place get it. They understand all sorts of details about how physical space works that so few understand. Have any of you been in your room with more than one person in it?"
Brenda: "Yes, it felt so small."
Silver: "Do you see how brilliant it is? Our rooms are perfect for one but crowded for two. That's all on purpose. The architects designed it for you to be okay being alone. Which can be hard if you're used to always having people around.

They have designed this place spatially to reflect what they
hope is going on psychologically while we're here."

Me: "Silver, you're so passionate about this."
Silver: "I am. I love it. I love to take a physical space like a
room or a building or whatever and get to its essence, figuring
out how to make it work for what people need it to be. But my
family just doesn't understand. They don't think my 'little
hobby,' as my mother calls it, matters. They don't think I
matter."

She starts to choke up again.

Sister: "Silver, is there any particular event that led you to the
H? Anything you'd like to share?"

Silver looks around at each of us. Her eyes rest on Sister the
longest. She then takes her left hand and grabs the end of her
right sleeve, which she pulls up to her forearm. She turns her
right wrist up so we can all see it. It's covered with big, two
and three inch long puffy, swollen gashes, the kind you get
from trying to slit your wrists.

K
Charis thinks this is crazy. She just rolls her eyes and says,
"Whatever, Mom…whatever." When I told her my idea, she

was against it from the beginning. But then I told her there's a huge mall near the airport.

Y

I really would like to get going on chapter one in Heschel's Book, but I can't get group out of my head. I'll find my mind wandering from Faruq's story to Kate's to Silver's to something Sister said to something Kate said...This is why it's good for people to go to work everyday. Otherwise, with all of this time on our hands, our brains get lazy. I don't know if it's because I'm not working or it's because this place is making me lose a firm grip on reality, but I can spend hours accomplishing nothing here. I've been in this chair in front of my room for two hours, and I'm just becoming aware that I haven't even read the first sentence. And those cut marks. When she pulled up her sleeve, I gasped. I couldn't help it. I consider myself a pretty good judge of people, but I never saw that coming. I wanted to call her dad right then and yell at him: How dare you! Let her be who she is! Quit shoving her into a mold! Stop pushing her to be something she's not! I keep reliving that moment. The shock of it. When I saw Faruq hug Brenda, I cried and cried. But when Silver pulled up her sleeve, that made me sad. Really, really sad.

But enough processing, I need to accomplish something.
Chapter one! What do you have for me, Abraham Joshua
Heschel?

"He who wants to enter the holiness of the day must first lay
down the profanity of clattering commerce, of being yoked to
toil. He must go away from the screech of dissonant days,
from the nervousness and fury of acquisitiveness and the
betrayal in embezzling his own life."

Profanity of clattering commerce? Yoked to toil?
The screech of dissonant days? Fury of acquisitiveness?
Embezzling his own life?

I am going to need's Dwight help.

R
I am so bored. Help me please, somebody. I am drowning in a
massive vat of boredom. The most exciting thing that may
happen today is that my seat covers are supposed to come in
the mail. How pathetic is that? I couldn't decide between the
light gray (they called it "Cold Steel Gray") and the "Sahara
Tan." It's so hard to tell on a laptop screen what the exact
color really is. Has it come to this? Looking out the window to
see if the truck is here yet? For seat covers?

K

Yves does this most of the days of the year? How awful. Just checking in was excruciating, let alone going through the security. And they took my unscented aloe vera body lotion! That's expensive stuff and they took it because it was in a four- ounce container and the limit is three. But the look on that security officer's face when I asked for his number and the name of his managing supervisor was great. You don't mess with the owner and president of Big Girl Lemonade.

V

I've seen this before. Beard? check. Sweatpants? check. Sandals? check. It's always the successful ones who lose all fashion sense when they crash. They go from dapper and sharp to stale and dumpy in no time. I'll bet this one is a CEO or something, maybe a record producer or a lawyer.

Y

This is going to be a joke. But I always tell people that they should be open to new experiences. When Sister said we'd resume group next week, it opened up all sorts of time in my schedule. Which I realize sounds ridiculous when I think about it. As if I have a schedule here. It's not like an hour or so every other day "opens up" a lot of time.

And speaking of time, time is different here. I don't really "do" anything and yet the days feel really, really full. To be honest, they fly by. I'll be sitting in my chair staring at the mountain and suddenly three hours have gone by. So lazy. I hadn't read the "Daily" sheet they put on the tables at breakfast because just processing Dwight and Sister and group has occupied most of my energies. But this morning I read it and it said there would be a Beginners Yoga class talk by "Vikki," and I was feeling a little adventurous so I decided to check it out. It was recommended that we wear "loose fitting clothing, or clothing specifically designed for yoga." Do sweatpants count?

V

Probably checked the Daily and saw Yoga and thought that as long as no one was watching, he should try it, you know, "branch out" and trying new things and all that.

Y

Oh God it's burning, Oh God it's burning, my groin is on fire, my groin is on fire, my crotch is full of needles…this is yoga? This is insane.

C

Are we seriously going to visit my dad at a mental place? How lame is that?

Y

I can't stop shaking. It's like I have no control over my body. Vikki said we'd start slow with something called Warrior One. Warrior One is kicking my ass. Why can't I stop shaking uncontrollably?

V

Nice. A bit of humbling going on. I know it's perverse of me to take pleasure in this, but who wouldn't enjoy it?

Y

I repent of everything I ever said about yoga being easy. I had no idea. I run almost every day, I'm in pretty good shape, but this has reduced me to a quaking mess in less than...what has it been?...Where's the clock...There's no clock? Why isn't there a clock? What does yoga have against the clock?

V

I usually start them out with a simple cat/cow, then some down dog, then some Warrior one, something to get them warmed up and breathing at a good pace. It's the easiest poses that often give people the hardest time...

Y

The first thing she told us to do was get on all fours for something she called "cat-cow." I almost laughed out loud. Cat-cow? My stereotypes were instantly confirmed. And so we arch our back like a cat and then bend the other way like a cow and she keeps reminding us to keep our breath consistent which is a no brainer—who doesn't keep their breath consistent all day long? Duh.

She then tells us that we're now going to enter into a series of vinyl somethings which involve a pose called "up dog" then one called "down dog" and then a "sun salutation" and I'm fine through the first one, it's basically a glorified push up followed by a hamstring stretch but it's on the second one and then the third one that it starts to burn. But it's a different burn. When I run I can feel the beads of sweat forming on my forehead after the second mile and by the third or fourth mile I'm drenched in a soaking sweat…

But in this vinyasa deal, the heat seems to come from the inside, like my intestines were in an oven. It felt like my skin got the heat message last, after the rest of my body, because when I started to sweat it was like a fog descended on my body. More like humidity than perspiration, if that makes any sense. And then, after several rounds of up and down dog, she has us stand still on one leg with the other leg resting on the inside of the thigh. Simple enough. But I started shaking and my groin started aching and my hands were trembling. Just standing there on one leg.

V

The moment it gets even slightly difficult for people to maintain a pose, the first thing they forget about is the breath.

Y

And then she reminds us to keep breathing. Which at the beginning sounded so dumb, like, of course we're going to keep breathing. But when she mentioned it again this time, I suddenly became aware that I wasn't breathing. Somehow, in the midst of the difficulty, I forgot the most basic thing. How long will this go on? I can't do it, I can't do it, I can't do it, I can't do it—there, we're done. She tells us to go into "child's pose," which involves folding my body in half with my legs under me and placing my forehead on the floor. Something so uncomfortable has never felt so good. I am like a limp rag, piled on the floor. I begin to find my breath. I sneak a look at my watch, lying on the floor next to my head. It's been 39 minutes.

And then, before I can stop it, something very, very bad happens. I pass gas.

V

Seen it, and heard it, a thousand times. It's always the successful ones, so accomplished and courageous and confident and yet so uptight, so driven, so compulsive. And few of them even realize it. This one? Just like all the rest. Give them a few minutes of focused breathing and simple movement and they lose control of basic bodily functions.

He's probably a runner.

K

The air. It's incredible. Five minutes breathing this desert air and I feel great. Like I've forgotten that we just spent four hours on a plane. Forget the A/C, I'm opening the windows.

Y

Sister and I are eating lunch together. I'm starving—a Cobb salad never tasted so good. My body is already sore.

Sister: "And how was yoga?"
Me: "Agony."
Sister: "You loved it that much?"
Me: "I had no idea. I thought it was for really flexible people."
Sister: "And you learned that it's for everybody…"
Me: "Is that a question? Because I did. I was a steaming puddle on my mat in a matter of minutes."
Sister: "It's actually easier for tighter people because they reach their edge faster."
Me: "Edge?"
Sister: "Everybody has an edge, the place where they reach their limit. A ballerina has an edge, just like a construction worker. They're just different. The one has to put her foot behind her head to feel something, and the other can try to touch his toes and break a sweat."
Me: "And that's why the teacher—Vikki, is that right?"
Sister: "Yes, Vikki."

Me: "Vikki mentioned how yoga has no room for competition."
Sister: "Oh my, don't get her started on competition! She has taught so many people who assume that yoga is like the rest of life-it's about winning. They get into her class and immediately start trying to figure out how to be the best, which is, of course, absurd. When they realize it doesn't work that way, it's very disorienting. It's not just different, it's like a new worldview."
Me: "I had a hard enough time just breathing."
Sister: "Amazing isn't it, that something so natural could suddenly be so difficult?"
Me: "I can't imagine what it would be like to breathe like that everyday. I'd be so relaxed. My body wouldn't know what to do!"
Sister: "So your work is stressful?"
Me: "Yes, very."

A little light is beeping on the dashboard of my mind, warning me to tread cautiously here. I'm Rue, not Yves. Can't give anything away...so I take a huge bite of salad and keep chewing for a long time.

Sister: "And how do you deal with the stress?"
Me: "Do you mean overall or in specific situations?"
Sister: "How about a specific situation. Tell me about something that happened lately, before you came here, and how you dealt with it."

Me: "Okay, here's one. I worked with my colleagues on a big project, and we recently found out that there may be a problem with the name of this project. We titled it in a different language, and it was brought to our attention that our translation may be a bit flawed."
Sister: "How was this brought to your attention?"
Me: "A man approached me who is fluent in the language of the title and tried to explain what he saw as the problem, but his English wasn't very good."
Sister: "How would you describe your interaction?"
Me: "It was tense. There were other people around, colleagues of mine, and I was stressed."
Sister: "And how did you respond to the tension?"
Me: "I did what I always do in situations like that—I tried to diffuse the situation and put everybody at ease."
Sister: "So what did you do?"
Me: "It's actually embarrassing, now that I think about it. There are a series of products associated with the project and I offered him some for free."
Sister (laughing): "Well, that's one way to deal with stress."
Me: "See! This is what is frustrating about you, and Dwight as well. You are so sharp and you ask such pointed questions that make me so uncomfortable, and yet when I confess to something horrible like offering somebody free stuff so he'll stop bothering me and go away, you laugh."
Sister: "It's funny."

Me: "But where's the judgment? The fingerpointing? You're laughing at me."
Sister: "And you can't laugh at yourself? If you lose the ability to laugh at yourself, Rue, you truly have lost your mind."
Me: "You think I've lost my mind."
Sister: "Not at all. But seriously, Rue, what was the real issue? Not the man standing in front of you accusing you of slaughtering his language, but the issue behind that issue. What made you tense?"
Me: "There were people watching—it was awkward. It wasn't the time for it."
Sister: "So if no one had been watching and it was just you and him, then you wouldn't have been tense?"
Me: "Good point. I would have been tense then as well. I would have offered him free stuff then, too."

I can't help but smile at this. Am I paying a thousand dollars a day for this?

Sister: "So it's not about the people watching. It's about something else. Enter into it."
Me: "How?"
Sister: "Enter in to the tension. Don't go around it. Go through it. Don't hand out free stuff. Don't do whatever it takes to make the man go away. Enter in to it. Like a room. If that moment was a room, go in to it and walk around and tell me what you see."

I sit still. I put my fork down. I breathe deeply. I give that moment everything I have.

Me: "Fear."
Sister: "What are you afraid of?"
Me: "I was scared he was right."
Sister: "And your fear led you to do what?"
Me: "I immediately did what I could to make it go away. It was too painful to consider that I'd spent all that money and time and effort to make something with such a big mistake in the name. Much easier to make it go away than to have to own up to it."
Sister: "Why?"
Me: "Too much at stake."
Sister: "Like what?"
Me: "I don't know….just a lot."
Sister: "Think about it—what was at stake? What was your real fear? The fear behind the surface fear?"
Me: "I know. I'd have to think about it."
Sister: "Then let's sit in silence and reflect on what that might be."
Me: "I don't like silence and I can't think of anything."
Sister: "Just sit in the tension."
Me: "I don't know—I couldn't understand him, it was an awkward encounter, people were watching..."
Sister: "And...? Keep going."

Me: "I don't know what you want. I'm not getting it."

Sister: "I think you are."

Me: "Enough with your tension and sitting in the silence and entering the moment. Enough! I give up."

Sister: "You give up?"

Me: "Yes, I'm done. I give up."

Sister: "That's a great place to be, isn't it?"

And with that, she stands up, pats the back of my shoulder, and leaves the table.

C

We have to what? Walk? Up the driveway? And it's almost a mile? What kind of a asylum is this? Only my dad would choose the weirdest freak show to hole up in and 'find himself.' And it had to be

in the desert, right? I'm going to die of heat stroke. Whatever.

Y

"I give up."

Did I just say that? Where is Yves Green? Who am I? I don't know if I've ever said "I give up." That's not who I am. Apparently Rue gives up. But Yves Green? Yves Green does not give up. He pulls himself up by his bootstraps. Because he has millones cojones. Right?

Khloe: "Hello, I'm here to visit my husband."
Bill: "He's a guest here?"
Khloe: "Yes. As far as I know."
Bill: "Would that happen to be him there?"

Y

I'm walking from lunch to my room, and as I walk through the courtyard I see Bill pointing at me from behind the desk. And he's talking to...Khloe and Charis.

C

My dad is crying. In public. And he can't stop hugging me and hugging mom and kissing my cheek and smiling and he has a beard. He looks awful.

K

I still don't know if this was a good idea. Besides the fact that I've never seen my husband cry, he looks like he's lost his bearings. And he's wearing the same sweatpants he left in. Who is this man?

Y

I don't know what's come over me. I can't get my emotions to behave. How embarrassing. I mean, I love my wife, and I love my daughter, but this is a bit over the top. Breathe, Yves, Breathe. And you too, Rue, you breathe, too. We all have to breathe.

Me: "How did you know who to ask for?"

Khloe: "What do you mean?"

Me: "When you came to the front desk, who did you ask for?"

Khloe: "I just said I was here to visit my husband."

Me: "Did you ask for me by name?"

Khloe: "No, I guess I didn't. The man at the desk just pointed and there you were."

Me: "So you didn't ask for me by name?"

Khloe: "No, I didn't. Why do you keep asking? Does it matter?"

Me: "Oh nothing—there's just a thing here with names. Never mind—let me show you around. Then maybe we can go for a family drive together."

K

What's wrong with Yves? I thought this place was supposed to help him. What's the deal with the names? Why all the questions?

C

Is anything more boring than driving around in the desert? My mom is at the wheel, and my dad is in the passenger seat, which usually drives him crazy. But neither of them have any idea where we are or what there is to do here in the middle of the nowhere. We must be hours from a mall or any kind of civilization. This sucks.

Y

I have no idea what to do. Or where we are going. I'm not even behind the wheel. But my wife and daughter are here. They missed me enough to come find me.

K

We've been driving for almost an hour, and I ask Yves if there's a park nearby.

Yves: "I have no idea."
Me: "What's that over there?"
Yves: "It looks like a sign of some sort, something about a National Forest area ahead."
Me: "Let's see what it is."
Yves: "I feel so bad that I don't have something planned for you guys. You surprised me and I didn't have time to cook something up."
Charis: "Like the time you 'cooked up' ten dancers dressed like Disney princesses crashing my tenth birthday party?"
Yves: "Kind of. Although I don't know where to find dancing princesses in the desert."
Khloe: "That was priceless. Or the time your dad had them announce at the Wiggles concert that it was your birthday and paid them to sing 'Happy Birthday' to you?"
Yves: "That one didn't go so well."
Charis: "It was terrifying. I ran out crying, didn't I?"

Yves: "That's what I mean by not going so well."
Khloe: "Check this out—it's a nature preserve."

Y

I can't ever remember Khloe wanting to hike. But we go and it's great. All sorts of twists and turns in the trail, and of course a million rocks and cactus. I have this nagging feeling of inadequacy because I have no connections out here. I don't know anybody. I can't pay somebody to do something amazing and surprising for Charis. No one has read my books or heard me speak. No one who owns anything or is connected behind the scenes to anything significant is offering to do me a favor because I am Yves Green, aspirational speaker. Just me and my ladies, walking in the wild.

Me: "Is anybody ready for a break?"
Charis: "Yes, my feet kill!"
Khloe: "There's a clearing. Let's stop."

We find this open space that has a little patch of green substance loosely resembling grass. Charis and I immediately lay down on it. Khloe reclines on a rock about thirty feet away. The clouds above strike me as being unusually "shapey"— waves and ships and horses and castles. Not that I've ever had the time to notice clouds.

Me (pointing): "That one looks like a buffalo."

Charis: "I can't believe I'm saying this, but it kind of does. Look at that one, reminds me of the top of a tree."

Me: "Or that one, it's like a puff of smoke from a cigar."

Charis: "Or those two—they're so long and straight, they remind me of tire tracks."

Me: "It's the jet stream of a plane."

Charis: "I know, that was a joke. You're so slow."

Me: "I am so slow."

Charis: "It's okay—you're a little crazy right now. How about that one? Looks like a man carrying a leaf."

Me: "And the one next to it looks like cotton candy."

Charis: "It kind of does."

Me: "Charis, do you think I'm crazy?"

Charis: "I don't know. Mom says you're getting a tune up."

Me: "Does she? What else does she say?"

Charis: "Not much. But it was her idea for us to come see you. She said 'a surprise visit was in order.'"

Me: "I agree. I'm bummed I don't have any great places to take you. I'm a bit out of my element here."

Charis: "Look at that one—it looks like that lamp we have in the living room."

Me: "It does. It really does. And that one looks like a bald man's head."

Charis: "Or a fat woman's shoulder."

Me: "I was just going to say that."

Charis: "You were?"

R

A late application for EXPLODE comes in the mail. It's from a young man who says that "Yves Green made me who I am today."

Y

I wake up. At some point Charis and I dozed off. At some point in the course of our nap, she put her head on my chest. I don't move. Khloe is still on her rock, reading a magazine she must have gotten from the car.

R

There's a question at the end up the application: "What do you hope to get out of the EXPLODE weekend?"
We purposely left it vague to see what people would write.
This guy writes: "My goal is to obtain the tools necessary to carry on the Yves Green tradition."

Tradition? There's a Yves Green tradition?

Y

I'm changing my clothes, and it's late. Khloe and Charis are probably at the airport by now. I'm tired and happy. I take off my shirt and see that there are pieces of grass all over the back of it. I hang the shirt up backwards on a hook. I climb into bed. I prop my head up so I can stare at the back of my shirt hanging there.

C

Rooster calls me tonight. He's concerned about Yves. I am, too. We have one of our most honest conversations ever. Noll says that everything will be fine.

Y

I climb up to the phone booth. I'm sure Khloe is back at work by now.

Khloe: "Hello?"
Me: "It's me. Good morning. I assume you made it home all right."
Khloe: "Yes, although flying is terrible. I can't believe you do this almost every day of your life. Awful. But yes, we're home."
Me: "You two surprised me. If I would have known I could have made some plans or pulled some strings, maybe cooked up something special for Charis."
Khloe: "I know, you said that when we were there. Several times. It's okay. We came to see you."
Me: "It's just new territory for me to feel so…helpless."
Khloe: "Do you know what she said on the way home?"

Me: "No."
Khloe. "Listen to me, Yves. We were sitting there waiting for our plane to board, and she was listening to her headphones. At one point she takes them off and she looks at me with total sincerity and says: "That was the best time I've ever had with Dad." And then she put her headphones back on."
Me: Stunned silence. "No way." More silence. "But all we did was lie on a patch of grass in the desert and watch the clouds."
Khloe: "That's right. And that's all she's ever wanted."

The rest of the conversation is a blur. I go back to my room and stare at the back of the shirt I wore yesterday. It's still hanging there on a hook. It still has grass on it.

R

Okay, okay, I know it's really pathetic. I admit it. I am aware of how it must look. I know that I was given what most people would die for—a month paid vacation to do whatever I want. But I'd already told them I'd be there. Besides, I already bought my ticket. That's how I rationalize it. Every year in Des Moines there's an event called LIFTOFF. It's like a turbo-charged conference for people who listen to motivational speakers. You buy one ticket for the four days and then you can listen to as many speakers as you want. I call it "The Buffet." If you time it right, you could literally be listening to somebody motivate and inspire you every moment of the day. And some people do.

In the early days, we dreamed of Yves being able to speak at LIFTOFF. When we finally convinced the organizers to give him an off-time on a side stage, he killed it. I'll never forget Lou coming to our hotel room after Yves spoke (we had to share in those days because we had no money), and in between huffs and puffs (because he'd run there, which is rare, to say the least) he explained they not only wanted Yves to come back next year and do the main stage, but there was a cancellation and they'd like him to fill in that night. Of course he stepped up and delivered. You could say he owes LIFTOFF because that weekend changed things for him. Which changed things for us. He's been in demand ever since.

So why am I going this year if Yves isn't speaking? Because it's one of the only events where all of Yves' competitors are in the same place at the same time. The green rooms have a sort of locker room vibe to them, everybody checking out the competition. You know, "How many books have you sold? How big are the rooms you're booking? Done anything in Europe?" It reminds me of when dogs meet and circle and smell each other's butts.

Y

Sister is back and so are the rest of us. There is a familiarity now that wasn't there several weeks ago (or was it a month ago? Or a year? I have totally lost track of time), and we chat freely about yoga and the food and Brenda's sun burn and Kate's snake sighting and how Faruq hikes before sunrise to the top of the mountain "just to get a good start to the day." It's nice.

Sister: "Well, there are still a couple of you who haven't had a chance to share. Steve, would you like to give us a bit of your story?"
Steve (still wearing the fanny pack): "Uh, I think I could probably do that. I get terrified in front of groups. Absolutely out of my mind scared. That first day when we were all in here I thought I was going to wet my pants. But then I didn't."

R

So yes, I go to LIFTOFF to check out the competition. But there's another reason as well. It was probably our third or fourth time, and there was a mix-up involving another speaker and who was on what stage at what time. So I ended up having to sort it all out with that speaker's logistics man, a great rotund chap named Paul Ortega who I liked the moment I met him. Paul handles the details for a speaker named Burt Buttrick. Picture John Madden crossed with John Goodman.

A big, bear-like American man. That's Burt. He's all about size. He wants everything bigger. One of his jokes is that FAMILY SIZE isn't big enough for him, and he wants companies to come out with TRIBAL SIZE.

So Paul and I were trying to figure out who goes on what stage at what time, and we're trying to make sure Yves is happy and Burt is happy and the organizers of the event are happy and the crowd is happy. We get it all sorted and Paul says to me: "Nobody knows what we do. The better we do our jobs, the less anybody notices? People only pay attention to what we do when we screw up!"

Finally, I thought, somebody I can relate to. I told Paul it was great to know somebody else who understands and he says, "You don't know about the Puff Club?"

Me: "The what?"
Paul: "The Puff Club. There's a whole group of us who do logistics for motivational speakers, and every year we get together at LIFTOFF and smoke really expensive cigars and tell war stories. It's a blast. Somebody said that you should be invited— has nobody got a hold of you?"
Me: "Uh, no. Why would they?"
Paul: "Are you kidding? You're Yves Green's right hand man. You're a legend. Tonight at the Winchester, 10 o'clock, okay?"

And with that, I was ushered into the inner circle of people who do what I do. That's really why I'm going to LIFTOFF.

Y

Steve continues: "Just sitting here, listening to you all has been so incredibly helpful. You'll never know. I came here wondering if there was any point to any of it—and I mean my life. Is there any point to any of it? But you've taught me so much about everything."

We have? Who knew? It's been great and everything, but Steve is the last person who looks like he's moved by anyone's stories. He always looks a bit preoccupied, like he cares about what's in that fanny pack more than anything else.

"But enough rambling. You know how you see trailers for movies—in theaters or online?" Trailers are big money. The studios pay literally millions to get the trailer just right because they know how many people will go see a movie based on their emotional response to the trailer. Have you ever noticed the voice that narrates them?"

Faruq (trying to sound like that voice): "'In a world where evil runs rampant, one narrator dares to describe it'—a friend and I have joked that it sounds like the same guy does all of them, you know, the one with that really dramatic, deep voice."

We smile politely at Faruq's attempt to relate. But Steve is not amused. Instead he sits straight up, sticks out his chest, tilts his head sideways, and booms: "'In a day and age ravaged by disease and war, in a land longing for hope, it's up to one man to find the heart and the will to stay and fight when all others have turned away in fear...'"

Holy shit. Steve is the movie trailer guy? Steve is the voice?

Steve then slumps back in his chair, his shoulders roll forward, and he transforms back into...the Steve we all know, who then says: "One and the same, Faruq. I'm that guy."

R

I can't believe I'm saying this but I like Des Moines. The airport is easy to get in and out of and the rental car people are good, heartland sort of people. It occurs to me as I leave the airport and head for the convention center that it might not be Des Moines that I'm particularly fond of. It might be the fact that I'm not at home sitting on my couch bored out of my mind, waiting on new accessories for my GTI to be delivered.

+++

Silver: "You're the voice in movie trailers?"

Steve: "Yes. It's the only job I've ever had."

Brenda: "Have you done any Brad Pitt movies?"

Steve: "Yes, I have."

Sister: "Well I'm sure we could ask Steve questions for hours, but I don't think he's here to answer questions about his work, are you Steve?"

Steve: "I guess I'm not, Sister. Work is actually my problem."

Sister: "Go on…"

Steve: "About three months ago, I noticed my throat was a little sore. I went to my doctor who did some tests. She told me I have an excessive build up of nodes on my vocal chords."

Kate: "Benign or…?"

Steve: "Benign, she thinks. It's developed over time. I talk for my job, and I have been talking for almost twenty-five years, every day all day. And to get my voice to sound like it does for recording trailers, I have to stress it. As you can see, I don't normally talk like that. That stress the doctor says will eventually cause me to lose my voice."

Silver: "So what does the doctor think you should do?"

Steve: "She's recommending surgery to remove them."

Brenda: "So what's the problem? Get the surgery, and get back to work! Have you ever met Meryl Streep? I just love her!"

Steve: "I've met with a number of experts on nodes and people who have had the surgery, and the general consensus is that the operation will change my voice. I may lose it altogether."

Faruq: "Which means you will have to find a new job."

Steve: "More than that. I am paralyzed by the thought of no longer being the movie trailer voice guy. It makes me catatonic. I just freeze. If I do decide to have the operation, I need to have taken a particular medication for a month to prepare my vocal chords. When the doctor handed me the bottle of pills, it felt like she was handing me poison. The bottle felt so heavy and dark and final. Like the thing I was holding in my hand could kill me. All day long I think about taking it and going through with the operation, and then I freeze and can't do it. I'll no longer be who I am…"

Me: "So you haven't taken the medication yet?"

Steve: "No. But I carry it with me everywhere I go, it's right here… in my fanny pack."

R

I've wanted to hear Rami Rez for a while. I read his book and I've seen his website, but there's no substitute for hearing a motivational speaker in a live setting. I'm impressed that he got the first morning slot of the conference on the main stage —a big deal for someone relatively unknown. That's actually part of the mystique of LIFTOFF—you never know who's going to get discovered there. The organizers have proven over the years they known how to spot the future stars. They gave Yves his big break.

The auditorium is full: people standing along the back walls, people on the floor. It's five minutes past the starting time when I hear "Is this on, is this on?" Somebody checking the mic. People quiet down.

Over the speakers comes the question: "Have you ever swam for your life?" Where is it coming from? Is this pre-recorded, or is someone talking live?

"Have you ever swam for your life, like if you didn't swim as hard as you could you might die? Because I have..."

He's in the crowd! He's two rows ahead of me! He stands up! Rami Rez was in the crowd the whole time, waiting for the event to start like the rest of us. And then he checked the mic and started talking. What a way to begin! The voice coming from the speakers was actually sitting among us the whole time. I have never seen someone do that. So unexpected. He continues:

"There's a small stretch of river on the border, that's the Texas-Mexico border for all of you gringos—"

We don't laugh. Can we laugh at that? Is the fact that we're gringos funny?

"You can laugh at that, by the way, all you gringos. I think it's funny, and I'm Mexican!"

Now we laugh. This is one fearless Mexican.

"There's this stretch of river where most of us crossed. Several of my cousins had done it a year before and so I knew it was possible but it's all talk until you're in the water and swimming for your life. Obviously, I made it. I hitchhiked to California because I'd heard there were jobs there. There weren't. I had no papers. No documentation. No driver's license. No birth certificate. No social security card. Everybody says: 'Just get a job, man.'"

He says it like Cheech and Chong, drawing out the word "man." The crowd loves it.

"But to get a job you need all those papers, and to get those papers you need a job. I tried to get a job with a lawn service, one of the bigger ones in L.A. I told the owner I would work for free until I was legal, just to prove how serious I was. I just needed somebody to give me a chance. They wouldn't hire me. I remember the day they told me no for the last time. I was standing out in the street in this really nice neighborhood, big houses with even bigger lawns, talking with the crew chief, begging him to let me work for free when he told me that he would never give a wetback like me a chance. He told me I should go back where I came from. He said, 'We're not a nation of immigrants—we 're Americans!'"

The crowd erupts. Rami Rez has them in the palm of his hand.

"Now I don't know whether I had rattled the crew chief and he just wanted to get away from me or whether they were late to get to another job, but he then jumped in his truck, yelled at his crew to load up and they sped off. It was then, standing in the street watching them drive away, crushed and defeated, that I saw that in their haste they had left something: one of their lawnmowers. Just sitting there on the sidewalk. So I took it, pushed it down the street, and started knocking on doors, offering to mow people's lawns for ten dollars less than whatever they were paying. Within two days I had ten lawns."

Rami Rez then walks towards the right side of the stage where there's something under a tarp I hadn't noticed until now. He yanks it off and there's a lawnmower.

"Here it is: that lawnmower. Eventually I sent a check for a thousand dollars to that crew chief. On the memo line, I wrote: 'Thanks for the lawnmower to help me start my business.'

Again, brilliant. People around me are eating this up.

"And so I mowed and I mowed and eventually I hired more help and after a year or so I applied to get my social security card and a driver's license. I'm standing there filling out the form and the line of people is long and the lines on the form are really confusing for a wetback like me—"

He winks as he says "wetback." Like we're all in on the joke.

"—where you put your first name and your last name, and so somehow I messed up and put part of my last name, which is Ramirez, on one line and part on another. So when I finally got my papers, they thought my full name was 'Rami Rez.' I figured I could live with it. Easier to live with it than go stand in line at the Secretary of State for another day or so."

Everyone is laughing and cheering. He's got them.

"Five years later I had four crews and three trucks, and by year seven I'd branched out into landscaping and pools, and by year ten I had made a million dollars. Do you know what I did with the money I made in those first ten years? I bought the house that I was standing in front of where I got that first mower."

Up on the screen behind him comes a picture of a beautiful house. Big, classic, brick with a huge lawn.

"I walked up to the door, knocked on it, and when the owner answered, I said: 'Ten years ago something very significant happened on the sidewalk in front of your house. I would like to buy this house and the sidewalk in front of it, how much do you want for it?'"

We cheer louder than ever.

"The question of course, is, do I mow my own lawn? I bet you're assuming that I have one of my crews do it. No way. I called that company that rejected me years ago and I hired them to mow my lawn. I even requested that particular crew chief because I had heard of his 'stellar reputation.'"

Up on the screen comes a picture of what I assume is the back of the house and the pool. Rami Rez is in the picture, relaxing in a lounge chair beside the pool while just behind him a man in a lawn maintenance uniform mows the grass. Rami is smiling at the camera, holding up a drink. It is priceless. It takes a while for the audience to settle down from this one. They cheer and shout and laugh and clap while Rami Rez just stands there. It appears to me, though, that he has more.

"You like that house?" We cheer some more.

"You love that picture of me sitting there with that man mowing behind me?"

We cheer even louder. "Can I tell you the truth?"

People are shouting "Yes" and "Go for it!"

"That's not what it's about."

The room gets really quiet really fast.

"It's not about how big your house is or how fast you can grow your business or how many cars you have. It isn't about what you can get. It's about what you can give. Several years ago I went back to the village I came from. The schools are in shambles, the drinking water is dirty, the soccer field doesn't even have goal posts. Here I am living in luxury in my new life while my village is in shambles. That's not right. I decided that it was time for me to do something with my life. Now I know some of you think that I have done something with my life, building a company, my house, all that. But that's nothing compared to what I'm up to now."

On the screen comes a picture of a partially constructed building. It's unclear what it's for.

"I know that you have lots of opportunities to spend your hard earned money. I've wandered around the lobby at events like this and seen every kind of piece of junk you could ever imagine with the speakers name on it or the name of his book. I've even seen beach chairs with the name of a book on it!"

Oh man, Rami Rez just took a swipe at Yves! This fearless
Mexican just slammed Yves Green in public. I am angry and
provoked, but my passions are tempered by the fact that I
always did have a problem with that beach chair.

"But that's not what I'm about. In the lobby you'll find no
trinkets with my name or the name of my book on them.
I don't want you to buy my stuff. I want you to help me make
life better for these good people living in a tough part of the
world. This is a picture of the school I'm building in the village
I'm from. If this school had been built when I was a boy, I
could have gotten an education and perhaps I never would
have had to leave. It's time for me to give back. And I'd love it
if you'd help me."

Up on the screen come pictures of Mexican children standing
in front of the partially constructed school.

"These kids need a school. They don't have one right now—"

A man stands up and yells: "I'll give you a hundred dollars
right now!" Another bolts up to the front of the stage holding
what looks like cash, another in the back yells, "Let's do this
Rami!" and on and on. Rami looks genuinely surprised. Is this
an act? Are these people he planted ahead of time? A man
three seats down from me stands up and yells, "I own a
construction company, and I'll send one of my crews for a

week for free!" People cheer at that one. Rami has what looks like tears in his eyes. He is either the best actor ever or this is real. And spontaneous. The crowd is caught up in it. Eventually he gains control enough to say, "Thanks."

He walks off stage to a thunderous, standing ovation. Only he doesn't walk off the stage to the green room area. He walks off the front of the stage into the crowd, where he starts shaking hands with the front row, and then the second row, and then the third row. It looks like he's going to shake every hand in the place.

Rami Rez is a contender.
And Yves Green is nowhere to be found.

Y
I decide to give Mr. Heschel another shot. I'm barely making sense of any of it when I come across this line: "Labor is a craft, but perfect rest is an art."

R
The more I think about what I just saw Rami Rez do, the more I think about Chuck Flannel. I am struck with the appalling thought that compared to the two of them, Yves seems kind of stale. Outdated, flat. I would never say that out loud, and

obviously I get my paycheck from Yves, but there is something
to their talks. It's more than that—it's their presence, their
aura, their purpose. I mean, have you ever seen a motivational
speaker ask for money so that he can give it to the poor? And
the crowd does it?

Y

After several paragraphs I don't understand, I come to this: "To
attain a degree of excellence in art, one must accept its
discipline..."

R

Ah, the Puff Club. This is one unique cast of characters.
Paul, my buddy who works for Burt Buttrick, and then there's
Sloan Major, he's the right hand man for a speaker named
Barbara Arabrab. Nope, not Slavik or Middle Eastern—her
name's a palindrome. Barbara was a school librarian for years
who discovered that she can do things with letters, like create
whole sentences that read frontwards and backwards the
same way, and she can talk spontaneously with each letter of
the sentence starting with the next letter of the alphabet.
Sounds odd, but she's amazing.

Sitting next to Sloan is Guy Parken, who left his job as an
accountant to run things for a speaker named Nigel. Nigel is

British and goes by one name. His latest book is FYT, which stands for "Find Your Thing." He says everybody has one thing they're supposed to do, and all you have to do is find that and everything will fall into place. I know how unbelievably simple that sounds, but Gary just told us that last week in Tampa, Nigel did four thousand in merch alone on one night. He said they sold out of the book in half an hour. People really are desperate.

Next to Gary is the lone woman in our group, Regina Fairson. Regina is a strong, loud, absolutely vivacious woman who is the right hand for Cliff Star. Cliff was a champion gymnast who, if you can believe this, wears tights and a tank top and does his whole speech using gymnastic equipment. He'll ask if anyone in the crowd can't do a handspring and of course almost every hand will go up. He'll then pick a random person and bring them up to teach them to do a handspring on the spot. It's actually quite powerful because he picks fat people and old people. And then somehow he teaches them and the crowd starts cheering them on and they're able to do it. He then talks about doing the impossible, not judging people by the outside, blah blah blah. Regina was just telling us how he's now teaching people back flips this tour.

Gary: "Don't you need them to sign some sort of waiver in case someone gets hurt?"

Regina: "Yes, we should. But no, we don't. Cliff says that would ruin his point. He says it's all about trust."
Paul: "It's all about trust until someone's lawyer calls! Is he still wearing gymnastic tights when he speaks?"
Regina: "Yes, and we're still trying to talk him out of it. But old ladies love it."
Sloan: "That's gross."
Regina: "You're not an old lady."

Do you see why I love the Puff Club?

Y

Sister and I are hiking again, and this time we go the opposite direction from our first hike. Away from the mountain, out into the valley where it is flat for miles in every direction. We walk in a straight line for hours. She asks me about my time with Dwight.

Me: "He gave me this book called The Sabbath."
Sister: "Ah yes, Heschel."
Me: "You know about him."
Sister: "Oh yes, he marched with Dr. King."
Me: "THE Dr. King?"
Sister: "Oh yes, The Reverend Martin Luther himself."
Me: "But I thought from the Sabbath title that Heschel was Jewish."

Sister: "You can't conceive of a Jewish rabbi marching for civil rights? Isn't that at the heart of what it means to be Jewish? Justice for everybody?"

Me: "Well, I don't know about that. I just wouldn't have thought…"

Sister: "Heschel's family was killed in the Holocaust which obviously informed the way he saw the world…"

R

Paul has just gotten done telling us about how Burt Buttrick has recently gotten in to the furniture business. He was in Boise giving a talk and when he made a joke about how he's tired of sitting in a "Lazy Boy"—he wants to sit in a "Lazy Man." So this guy walked up afterwards and said he owns a factory and would love to help Burt design and manufacture a Lazy Man chair. Apparently Burt is on this kick that if you're going to be lazy, be really lazy. Go the whole way. He was complaining that the lever on the side that raises the footrest is just too much work, so his new chair will have a voice-activated footrest. So you don't even have to use your arm to raise it up. We all roll our eyes. Paul thinks it's ridiculous, too.

Regina: "Rooster, what's the deal with Yves canceling?"
Someone finally points out the elephant in the room. Knew it was coming.

Me: "You know, Regina, I have two answers."

Regina: "And they are…"

Me: "The first is because of the EXPLODE weekend coming up."

Gary: "I've heard about that. Takes balls to attempt something like that."

Sloan: "Don't you mean it takes 'millones cojones'?"

Good one, Sloan.

Me: "Yves told us he wants to do nothing but concentrate on getting ready for that. Which meant I had to make all the cancellations."

Paul: "Oh, I hate those. When Burt had his first heart attack, I had to make those calls. Hated it."

Me: "The other answer is…well, I just don't know. I don't get what he's going through. Maybe it's like a midlife crisis or something."

Regina: "Actually, whatever it is, it's probably quite normal. Do any of you ever watch your boss doing what they do for the hundredth time and wonder where they find the motivation to keep going?"

Gary: "All the time. Nigel has this new story he's been telling that takes forever. It's about Margaret Thatcher and a showdown she had with a workers union, and it involves all of these details about contracts and wages and politics. I don't think his American audiences understand half of it, but he tells it every night. And it takes forever and it exhausts me just to hear it. And yet he goes for it every time, like it's the first time he's ever told it."

Sloan: "I sometimes think you have to have something seriously wrong with you to be a motivational speaker."
Paul: "I'll drink to that." And we do.

Y

Sister and I are now walking along a dried up riverbed.
Me: "I didn't get anything Heschel was saying at first, but when Dwight explained it, it started to click. The parts about time at least."
Sister: "How so?"
Me: "Well, in my work I stick to a schedule. I finish a job and then I move on to the next one. And then the next one. And then the next one. Everything for me is about time."
Sister: "So what do you do after a big project is completed?"
Me: "I get ready for the next one."
Sister: "I meant, how do you relax, decompress, how do you unwind?"
Me: "I work out, I read emails, nothing much."
Sister: "Why do you work out?"
Me: "Why? It feels good. It gives me energy. I don't know— lots of people work out. It's not that unusual."
Sister: "Yes, lots of people do, but why do you? Because it gives you energy?"
Me: "Yes, among other things."
Sister: "And what kind of emails are you reading?"

Me: "They're mostly from people who have benefitted from the work my organization does."
Sister: "And how do those make you feel?"
Me: "They're a rush! They're like pure adrenaline. They make it all worth it."
Sister: "Do you see a connection?"
Me: "A connection? Between...?"
Sister: "Between the various elements of your life."
Me: "I know enough to know you're getting at something deeper here, but again, I'm missing it."
Sister: "Your work is a rush. Your workouts give you a rush. Your email gives you a rush."
Me: "Right—it's a great life!"
Sister: "Is it?"
Me: "Well, I'm here, so obviously it isn't."
Sister: "When do you stop?"

R

I am on my third Rob Roy. It's such a great drink. That's why I order it. It's so much better than saying, "I'll have a beer." Anybody can say that. But to nod to the waitress and say, "Rob Roy please." That's class. So I'm on my third Rob Roy when Sloan says "By the way, I invited someone new to join us tonight..."
Gary: "And who would this be?"
Sloan: "Have any of you heard of Chuck Flannel?"

Me: "Oh man oh man—"

Regina: "You've heard him?"

Me: "He's awesome! I heard him and then we went backstage and met him. He has one leg."

Paul: "Chuck Flannel has one leg?"

Me: "Yes, but it's better if you don't know that when you go to hear him. It makes it all the more impressive. He'll blow you away."

Sloan: "Great, glad to hear it because, the spec sheet for the conference said his logistics are handled by someone named Feeb so I sent him a text with an invite."

I try to play it cool. Just sippin' my Rob Roy, no big deal.

Gary: "And you've met this Feeb, Rooster?"

Me: "Yes, I've met her."

Y

Sister: "It appears as though you move from one high to another."

Me: "And what's wrong with that?"

Sister: "When do you come down?"

Me: "Down? Why would I want to be down?"

R

"Rooster?"

I turn around. "Hi, Feeb."

Feeb: "I didn't know you'd be here. I thought since Yves cancelled you wouldn't be at the conference."

Me: "And I had no idea you'd be here. I didn't know your dad was speaking..."

Feeb: "He wasn't until they invited him to take Yves' spot. They told us you'd recommended him when you called to cancel."

Me: "Of course—Chuck blew us away. It's great to see you again. Let me introduce you to everybody."

We make our introductions and begin lighting the cigars—Cubans smuggled in courtesy of Gary, via Nigel.

Regina: "So tell me about Chuck Flannel."

Feeb: "He's something. He's also my dad—did Rooster tell you that?"

Gary: "Chuck Flannel is your dad? You work for your dad?"

Feeb: "He's great. It works really well. You never know what's coming next."

Sloan: "I've heard some amazing stories about him. Is the stick story actually true?"

Feeb: "The Oval Office one?"

Sloan: "Yes, that one! Did that actually happen?"

We all want to hear this story. Which Feeb tells. I don't know which is better, the story, or simply staring at Feeb, and because she's telling a story, I can stare all I want. Apparently, Chuck is a big fan of the President and has always wanted to meet him. So someone who knows the two of them set up a meeting in the Oval Office. At the time of the meeting, the President was dealing with a tense situation involving the president of a nation I can't pronounce and a terrorist group that has it's headquarters in that country. So our President was meeting with this other president the next day to convince him to turn over the terrorists for trial. Chuck Flannel insisted on carrying a walking stick with him into the White House, and no one thought anything of it because he has one leg. When he got into the Oval Office and shook the President's hand, Chuck slammed the stick down on the President's desk and said: "Mr. President, stick it to 'em!"

We howl. We pound the table. We love this story. We love Feeb. Okay, I love Feeb.

Y

I'm actually starting to find little bits in Heschel that jump out at me. It's like a whole new way of reading. I used to be the master skimmer. I attack books for the purpose of getting through them. Like they're the forest and I'm in a plane, and I skim the tops of the trees. But this, this Heschel fella, I can't fly over his book. It only means something if instead of passing over it I dig though it. I come across this:

"The world has already been created and will survive without the help of man."

R

There are a thousand reasons why I am crazy about Feeb. One of them is watching everybody else go crazy about Feeb. Obviously the men think she's beautiful. But Regina clearly likes her, too. Or maybe I should say respects her. Feeb carries herself in a certain way that demands respect. She has a dignity about her. She knows who she is. That's it. She isn't clingy, she isn't desperate. So many women are looking for something—validation, worth, the perfect guy. It's like they're looking for a man to give them something they're missing. Feeb isn't missing anything. And she's hot. Did I mention that?

Y

Heschel keeps talking about the Sabbath, which I'm gathering is Saturday. I think. It has something to do with one day a week. That's pretty clear. As if anything in Heschel's writing is "clear." He writes that the Sabbath "is a day for the sake of life." So it's a day, but it's something more. It's like a place, but

not in physical space, but a place in time. If that makes sense.
"It is the result of an accord of body, mind, and imagination."

R

And then Feeb stands up, thanks everybody for the invitation
and the drink, and says goodbye.
Me: "What? You're leaving?"
Feeb: "Yep, I'm no good after ten. But I'm killer at sunrise."

And with that she turns and leaves.
Do I follow her? Do I stay at the table? Do I beg her to stay? I
am paralyzed. And she is gone.

And I am buzzed. Is it from the Rob Roys? Or is it from Feeb?
The answer is yes.

Y

Heschel tells this story about a prince who's in captivity and
lives anonymously among rude and illiterate people. His father
sends secret word to him not to forget the ways of a prince
because someday he will send for him. So the prince invites
everybody to the local tavern and buys them food and drink
because, Heschel says, the soul cannot celebrate alone.

The first time I read the story I got hung up on the details: What kind of father sends his son away and then brings him back later? How is that captivity? Why didn't the father just set him free? Why did he have to live with rude and illiterate people?

The story made no sense. But what I've learned with this book is to read it again. And then read it again. Don't fly, dig. And so I read it, again. And again. And again. The story is like a trance for me. I enter in to it. And I read it again. And again. And again.

R

That night Feeb is in my dream. She is wearing a lab coat. It is, unfortunately, a modest lab coat. Which, in an odd way, makes her even more alluring. I swear those Victorians were on to something. But she is not in my dream for that reason—she is in my dream because she has work to do. I know this right away because she is holding her clipboard. It is the sexiest, most erotic clipboard in the long and distinguished history of clipboards. She is standing in water up to her knees on the beach at Witch's Rock in Costa Rica. As you'll recall, I have some history there.

Behind her I can see trees which tells me that I'm out farther in the water, looking back at her. But I can't see her very well, and she keeps fogging up. Which I realize isn't her—it's something on my head. I'm wearing some sort of helmet, and I can hear her talking like she's in my ear. Apparently there's a speaker inside the helmet I am wearing, which also must have goggles or something. That's it. Now I get it. I keep fogging up my goggles because I'm trying to say something to her, but I can't get the words to make any noise. She is telling me something, and she is very insistent about it, leaning forward, reading off of her clipboard, repeating something again and again. I begin to hear her faintly at first, but louder and louder until her voice is booming in my ears: "Rooster, your problem is not the salt water. Your problem is not the salt water."

Funny, dreams.

Y

I have questions. I start writing them down. But when I write a question down, it triggers all sorts of thoughts, which I then write after my question. And then I write the next question down which triggers thoughts about that question and the one before it and the thoughts I had after the first question. I am writing furiously. I go back after filling five pages and read it. Some of it is gibberish, and some of it only raises more questions. Which I write down. I read it all through again because my hand has cramped. At the top of page four I read what I had just written:

Chuck Flannel and his dining room table made out of that tree. Inviting Greg Dodge to dinner. Was this because the "soul cannot celebrate alone?"

R

My head aches. My heart aches. I have a hangover from four Rob Roys. I am a serious lightweight of a drinker. I am riding the elevator from the tenth floor to the lobby. It stops at the seventh floor and a man gets in. He is wearing a "What's Your Deal?" hat. Ah yes, Eddie Maroni. Eddie Maroni is speaking on the main stage today. He was a used—excuse me, "pre-owned"—car salesman for years. A legend in the business. I heard him tell a crowd in Reno he started with "two Mustangs and thirty feet of concrete," and "now I sell thirty Mustangs a day without moving two feet on the concrete." His new book is called What's Your Deal?

His central premise is that everybody needs a deal, a thing to give themselves to, a cause, a mission, and that without one we're wasting our lives. Basic motivational speaker talk.

But Eddie's different because he's an organizational genius. His content is as basic and bland as it gets, but he knows how to get people involved and how to organize volunteers. I had heard that he was trying something new at LIFTOFF this year,

something about a volunteer army. This guy in the elevator is obviously part of "Eddie's Army." Not only is he wearing the "What's Your Deal?" hat, he's wearing a "What's your Deal?" golf shirt with the logo on the pocket, a nylon bracelet with WYD? on it and—oh, this is classic—he's got a WYD? backpack in which to carry all his other WYD? stuff. Then I have an epiphany. I am thinking about how lame this guy is and how he needs to get his own life instead of being a shill for Eddie Maroni when the elevator stops at the third floor and he gets off. The elevator walls have mirrors on them. Which means I can now see a reflection of myself where he was just standing. I see my bag, sitting at my feet. It says on it "Millones Cojones." I am wearing a windbreaker with "Bootstraps" printed on the chest above my heart.
It's time to leave this place.

Y

I run up the mountain. I arrive at Dwight's rock out of breath. I am so fired up to talk with him but I'm embarrassed because my lungs burn. I smile and point to my chest and he smiles and says: "You'll get used to it, if you stay here for a year or so."

He thinks this is hilarious.

Me, finally: "Can we talk more about Heschel?"

Dwight: "I thought you'd never ask."

Me: "I'm starting to get it. To get him."

Dwight: "You think so?"

Me: "But it's different from other books. Other books you read and the person tells you something, and you either didn't know it or you did and you file it away and agree or not or whatever and then you're on to the next page. With Heschel, it's like you don't read—it reads you. It's like being in a room filled with exotic pieces of art and you have to walk really, really slowly because there's just so much hanging on the walls."

Dwight: "Give me an example."

Me: "The story about the prince. At first I dismissed it because it doesn't make any sense."

Dwight: "You're talking about the king sending word to his son? Why was the son sent away in the first place? Why didn't his dad just send for him right away?"

Me: "Yes!"

Dwight: "And while we're at it, why is he living with 'rude and illiterate people'?"

Me: "Exactly! The story is absurd. And if you stay at the surface level, caught up in the mechanics of it, the story stays distant and absurd. So I read it again and then I read it again and it started to do something to me."

Dwight: "You entered into it."

Me: "Yes, I entered in. And I started to feel it. Like I was the prince buying everybody drinks and food. And I started to see that I'm not the prince, but I want to be. I've never learned the ways of the kingdom. I started thinking about some things that happened before I came here, and suddenly this arcane story about a confused king and an exiled prince started to be about me. It affected me. Deeply."

Dwight: "And this, Rue, is what the philosopher Ken Wilber calls the difference between 'translation' and 'transformation.'"

Me: "Wait—you're losing me."

Dwight: "No, it's actually quite simple. Translation is simply taking something from one place and putting it another. People hear something they like and they take it and put it somewhere in their lives where it fits, where there's room, where things like that are supposed to be—and on they go. But transformation-transformation is when you hear it or experience it, and it goes to work on you and you come out the other side a different person. There's a distinction here, and the two can often look similar, especially with something like religion, but they're night and day."

Me: "And that's me and the prince?"

Dwight: "It appears so to me. You could have read that story and when I asked you what it meant to you, you could have said: 'Well, we should include people and be generous with our money and make sure we host parties on occasion.'"

Me: "Just repeating clichés that I already know—"

Dwight: "Precisely. But this story captivated you because you let it. And you found yourself in it. That line about the 'soul can't celebrate alone' is about your soul, isn't it?"

Me: "For some reason the table and eating—maybe I should say 'the meal' has become a big issue to me. Most of my meals have something to do with business. I'm with the people I work with, and we're talking about business, the next project, what's coming up, what these people want me to do for them. The more important the project, the nicer and more expensive the restaurant. Meals have a point for me. They always have. But I recently met this man who was telling me how he has this big table and he invites all of his family and friends to eat at it and there wasn't really any point, other than all of them being around that table.

Dwight: "Did you catch Heschel's line about the 'inefficiency of the Sabbath'?"

Me: "Yes, I did."

Dwight: "Because that's what you're talking about. You're saying your meals are "efficient," they're accomplishing something, they're about something else. They have a point beyond themselves. You use the meal for something other than the meal itself."

Me: "Right, I do. But there was this moment before I left with my family when I invited this boy who likes my daughter to go out to eat with us. I shocked everybody—including myself. I don't do spontaneous nights out. I realize now that what I wanted was to be rescued from efficiency. From getting things done. That fact that inviting him had no point other than celebrating being together. There was no other point!"

Dwight: "Freeing, isn't it? It's not that you can't get together to eat and actually get something done..."

Me: "Which takes me back to the Prologue where Heschel talks so much about time—and that helps me understand why he keeps mentioning this Sabbath thing. We can become slaves to efficiency to such a degree that we don't know what to do with time other than get things done with it."

Dwight: "Yes! On that note, tell me about your days off."

Me: "When I'm not working, all I'm really doing is recovering from the work I did and ramping up for the next round of work ahead."

Dwight: "Here—read the part about 'Menuha.'"

Me: "Okay, good because I found that menuha concept really fuzzy. Here it is: 'Menuha is more than withdrawal from labor and exertion...It's more than freedom from toil, strain or activity.'"

Dwight: "Great, isn't it?"

Me: "Explain."

Dwight: "He's saying there is another state beyond the two states of work and not working. Menuha is that place of... what are his words?...'stillness and peace and harmony.' Sabbath is not just a day off, a day of not doing something. It's not defined by what it's not. People take a day off and they're no better the next day."

Me: "Which is why you asked me if my time away from work is really all about work as well..."

Dwight: "Well said. Sabbath isn't just not working. It's about entering in to the peace and calm and life and energy and vitality at the center of the universe."
Me: "Ahhhh...and that's why he says that Sabbath is about how the universe doesn't need man's energy to exist."
Dwight: "We take one day a week to remind ourselves that the world does not exist by our effort."
Me: "Because it's moments that lend significance to things, not things to moments!"
Dwight: "Heschel would be thrilled to hear you say that, Rue."

R

I call Claudia from the airport. We talk for a while. She agrees. She asks Noll while I'm still on the phone with her. Noll's in. She buys their tickets. I change mine.

Y

I wake up with a terrifying thought. Today is group and everybody has shared but me. I lay in bed and feel the old pit forming again in my guts. It's been a while since the pit was here. The pit is back. Do I make up a fake story? They're too smart, and they'll figure it out. Could I lie to Kate? No way. Faruq? Nope. Sister? No chance. Do I come clean? Do I tell them the true story but change just a couple of the details so I'm still Rue?

Here we are. I know it's totally clichéd to say these people feel like family, but Sister was right that first night—there is a family thing that kicks in. I have a sort of big brother impulse towards Silver, and even Steve has become a tragic yet endearing kind of guy and Faruq is...Faruq. He never stops inviting me to climb the mountain with him at sunrise, and I never stop telling him that people with beards wearing sweatpants don't climb things. He laughs at that and I laugh at that, and then the next time I see him he asks me again. Sister shows up and we're all chatting and the pit in my stomach is yelling at me and I know that at any moment Sister is going to call on me. I need help. I need a miracle.

And then I get it.

I see some people walking through the lobby, looking around like they're lost. It takes me a second to realize it's Rooster and Claudia and Noll. I jump out of my chair and knock it over, and everybody immediately thinks something is wrong but I say over my shoulder, "No, it's great, everything's great—it's just that my friends are here!"

And I bound out of the room. I have no idea if my miraculous rescue and the ensuing relief are the source of my joy or that my staff have come across the country to see me. I come around the corner and stretch out my arms to give Rooster a hug.

R

I knew this place was mental. I knew it was for crazies. We're walking around looking for Yves and some Grizzly Adams dude comes around the corner and tries to hug me. There's no way Yves would even stay in a place like this for one night, let alone however many weeks it's been.

Y

Rooster backs away.

Me: "Hi, guys!" They look stunned.
Me: "What's up? Miss me?" They don't say anything.
Me: "It's me. Yves."

R

The image that races into my brain is of my parents' basement. Because this is Yves standing in front of me. But it's not Yves.

He gives us each a hug. Claudia and Noll are speechless. Open-mouthed, jaw-dropping speechless.

Yves: "How did you find me?"

Me: "I called Lou."

Yves: "He told you?"

Me: "He just said you'd asked about the Hesed House."

Yves: "Amazing! And how did you know where to find me once you got here?"

Me: "We didn't. There was no one at the front desk so we walked right in and looked around and then there you were..."

Yves: "So you didn't ask for me by name?"

Me: "No, why?"

Me: "Never mind. Rooster, you are amazing."

Me: "It's what I do, Yves."

Y

They came all the way here to surprise me? What do they want? I'm glad to see them, but not so sure they were glad to see me. At least, the me they expected to see.

R

We're seated in the eating area. It's empty except for us.

Me: "We have some very exciting news—Noll, show him."

Noll: "Now remember, we can still changes things, but we're thrilled so far..."

Y

Noll has something in his bag he's trying to pull out, and when he does I see it's a bunch of...golf shirts. He pulls one out that has the word "EXPLODE" across the chest with little pieces of shrapnel drawn all around it.

I don't say anything.

Claudia: "Well...what do you think?"
Me: "That's a shirt all right."

I realize at this moment that I have blown it. I've let them down. These people who have given me the majority of their energy and waking hours for the past several years have flown across the country to see me and support me and show me a shirt design they're thrilled about for an upcoming event we created together.

And all I can muster is "That's a shirt all right."

R

I don't think our visit ever recovered from that moment when Yves saw the shirt design. It was clear things would never be the same. This man was no longer Yves Green. This man couldn't tie his shoelaces—well, actually that's true since he

was wearing sandals—let alone pull himself, or anyone else,
up by their bootstraps.

Y

I apologize for not being enthusiastic enough and repeat over
and over what a great shirt design it is, but I've lost the ability
to fake it and things are just way too strange between us.
They're trying to figure out who I am and what I'm doing here
and where this is all headed. And so am I.

R

There is a moment at the end of our conversation when we tell
him we need to get back to the airport. I know no one else will
ask so it's up to me: "So Yves, when are you coming back to
work?"

Y

They must be wondering about their jobs. This thought occurs
to me just before I realize that none of us has said the word
"EXPLODE" yet. So I say it. Even though it feels like somebody
else's life. Someone else's event.

"Don't worry about EXPLODE. I'll be there."

R

I'm relieved to hear Yves say he'll be at EXPLODE. I can't imagine having to cancel that. But it also raises a more important question: Who will be there? Yves Green or Grizzly Sweatpants?

Y

I am laying on my bed staring at the back of my shirt hanging there with the grass still on it. The pit is back and bigger than ever. I begin to wonder if I've been living a fantasy. Like I took a free pass from life for a while and today, with the visit of my staff, I have suddenly and violently been reminded that there is a world out there and I have a role to play in it. A role that has already been decided. One I don't have much say in.

I feel trapped. Claustrophobic. Being Yves Green is like being in a closet where there is a shortage of fresh air. My identity is choking me, suffocating me, cutting off my air supply. Here I can at least breathe again.

EXPLODE is a few weeks away, and I have been avoiding this fact for weeks now, up on the side of a mountain in the desert miles away from my problems. I lay here realizing that I have more anxiety about staying than going. I can't avoid it. Dwight has been enlightening and Sister is charming and group is moving, but that's not how I get to live, thinking and reflecting and living so slow and lazy. I have a decision to make.

R

Leaving Des Moines was surreal because of that guy in the elevator but leaving Arizona is awful. Not that I want to stay. It's just that I don't know what I'm going home to. I don't know what "home" even is. I can't imagine that the Yves we just saw is in any condition to EXPLODE. Not in any good way.

Y

I wake up knowing that it's time to leave. I go to the front desk and ask for Sister, who I'm told is still at breakfast. I find her and tell her that it's time for me to leave. I'm expecting her to tell me that I have a lot of work to do and I'm only cheating myself if I leave now. But she doesn't.

Sister: "I understand. If it's time, it's time. I only ask one thing of you, Rue."
Me: "After all you've done for me, no problem."
Sister: "You need to climb the mountain before you go."
Me: "Faruq's mountain?"
Sister: "It's not Faruq's, it's ours. It's everybody's. And I think you should climb it before you leave."
Me: "All the way?"

Sister: "To the top."

R

Yves calls me and tells me he's coming home in a few days.
Without thinking, I quickly say: "Oh good, then things
can return to normal." But then I stop and ask how he's doing
and if he feels better and when he wants us to pick him up at
the airport. I know things will never go back to normal.

Y

Faruq does this every morning? I've been hiking for hours and
I'm nowhere near the top. How early does he leave and still get
back for group? My mind races. I think about Faruq and his
son and Silver and Khloe and EXPLODE and a thousand other
things. I picture Heschel walking alongside Martin Luther King
down some street in the South, and there are people yelling
and cursing at them and they march on. I march on up the
mountain, believing that there is some reason for this
madness. The madness of canceling all of those gigs, the
madness of confusing my wife, the madness of checking in to
the H, the madness of sitting there with Dwight discussing
things I don't understand.

The wind blows stronger and stronger the closer I get to the
top, and the sun beats down as I walk in a sort of trance. I feel

unstable. Trapped and claustrophobic, confined inside the life of a man named Yves Green. A man I barely know.

I make it to the top. There is a wood bench. It is the most comfortable piece of furniture I have ever sat on in my entire life. I take in the view. Birds ride the swirling wind currents around me. The desert canyon sprawls all around me. I am dizzy and thirsty and desperate. I beg the universe for inspiration. I need something. A piece, a fragment, something to save me from the despair that is orbiting me with the birds. I lay down on the bench. I doze off. I wake up. I doze off again. I remind myself to breath. I try to act like Sister, calm and aware and fully present. I try to slow the images that are coming and going from my mind. The word "lose" keeps coming up, as does "give up" and "die." Little snippets from Heschel loop in my mind,

"time is the heart of existence" and
"it's not things that lend significance to time..."

and none of them make sense and yet they're familiar, helpful even.

Images of Dwight dancing and Silver's legs and hugging Rooster and Kate's smile and Bill talking about a plate of pasta he had in a bistro somewhere near the Sistine Chapel.

It is somewhere in this fog of despair that it comes. I do not
think it up. I do not create it. It arrives fully formed. I do not
shape it into something comprehensible. That's how I get it.
Complete. Finished. Ready. Waiting.
I get up from the bench.
I run part of the way down the mountain.

Y

Me: "Hello?" "Rooster, it's me, Yves."
Rooster: "Yves? Hey."
Me: "Can you talk?"
Rooster: "Yes. Yves, are you okay?"
Me: "Yes, I am. Never been better. I have an idea, Rooster, a
big idea and I'm going to need your help."

R

He almost sounds like the old Yves I used to know—the guy
who would call me any time of the day or night with a question
about what snacks I'd ordered for the green room in Fresno or
to see what I thought about printing up iTunes gift cards with
his photo on them. Maybe I'm dreaming again…

Me: "What kind of idea? For EXPLODE? Or…?"
Yves: "Well, kind of a saving idea. That's probably not the best
word. It's an idea that comes from somewhere else, and it

came to me just now at the top of the mountain and we have
to do it."

Me: "We do?"

Yves: "Yes, and I'll need you and Noll and Claudia. I can't do it
without you."

R

I call Noll. I ask him to get Claudia on the other line. I tell them
about the call I just received from Yves. They are
dumbfounded. I share with them the idea. Claudia keeps
repeating, "This is crazy." Noll gets really excited and insists
that it's totally possible. He wants to get started.

Y

I say my goodbyes. It is agonizing. I embrace Kate after
breakfast and she tears up and I hug Brenda and Silver and
Steve and we exchange emails and Faruq puts his arm around
me and tells me he'll miss me. I leave my room and see Bill on
the way out who smiles his Bill-smile and tells me it's been an
honor to have me there. I am torn up inside. Wrecked.

But I promised Sister I would meet her out front to say
goodbye before I got in my taxi. I have a lump in my throat. I
am working very hard to keep it together when I see her. Tears
are right there, waiting to come racing down my face.

She shows up wearing a "Subvert the Dominant Paradigm"
t-shirt. She has something tucked under her arm. While
I am all emotional and mushy and overwhelmed with the
moment, it occurs to me that she probably says goodbye to
people all the time as they're leaving here. It is, after all, her
job. This helps me maintain control. Knowing that it's part of
her job to say goodbye, and it's not that unusual or special
helps puts the moment in proper perspective.

Sister: "Well, I guess this is it. It's been a pleasure having you
here."
Me: "I can't begin to thank you for everything. "
Sister: "There is one thing I would like you to do for me before
you go."
Me: "Anything. You name it."

She takes whatever it is from under her arm and hands it to
me. It's a copy of the Bootstraps video, the one she played at
the beginning of that first group.

She smiles and hands me a marker. "Could you please sign
this for me?"

Wait. What? No. Can't be.

No way no way no way no way no way no way. She just
stands there and smiles. Does she…? Did she…? Did she

know who I am all along? The mountain and the valley and the taxi spin and I feel so disoriented.

What?

Sister says: "Years ago I was married. He was an angry man who hit me and betrayed me and eventually I found enough strength to leave him. Our kids were in their teens at the time and they came with me. We had nothing. I found us an apartment, and I worked three jobs. When I wasn't working or taking care of my kids, I spent the time hating him. One of my jobs was cleaning a community center. I would spend entire night shifts on my knees, all alone, scrubbing the bathroom floors, ruminating on my hurt and anger and repulsion for what this vile man had done to our family. One evening I was waiting in the back for that night's program to end so I could vacuum the aisles when something the young man on the stage said grabbed me. It was some sort of inspirational event, sponsored by the local Rotary Club, and they had brought in an up-and-coming motivational speaker for the evening. He was so young and innocent and energetic. What caught my ear was when he said, 'You don't have to be a victim if you don't want to be.'

"I sat down in the back in one of the empty seats. I hadn't heard this before. I listened to the rest of his talk. I don't remember a thing he said after that. But when he was done, I stayed in my chair. I asked myself what I was going to do with my life. Then I remembered the proverb my grandmother used to quote me whenever someone would do something strange or hurtful or inexplicable. She'd shake her head and say, "The waters of a person's soul run deep." Something about that resonated with me, even as a young girl. I had this awareness that my job was to help people swim in those waters. I was put here to help people understand why we think and feel and act the way we do. Sitting in the back of that community center auditorium, exhausted, wounded, burdened down with the weight of the world, I decided that I would go to college and then I would go to graduate school and I would become a counselor and nothing would stop me. And nothing did. I ended up going to the same college as one of my kids—at the same time! We even had a class together!

Which brings me to this moment. For seventeen years very few days have passed in which I have not thought to myself, 'Some day I will find a way to thank that young man for what he said that day that changed my life forever.'

And now, today, I get to."

And with that, she hugs me, she backs away, she looks at me with an ocean of compassion in her eyes and she says,

"Thank you, Yves Green. Thank you."

I am numb. I just stand there, holding that marker and that
DVD.

Me: (After a long silence): "So it was a setup?"
Sister: "A set up?"
Me: "You played that video in group to get under my skin
because you knew it was me?"
Sister: (Tilting her head back and laughing one of those
nuclear laughs of hers.) "Of course not! That's crazy.
I had no idea you were in the group. I always play that clip
when we have new people."
Me: "You do?"
Sister: "Yes…it always provokes people. It always gets a
reaction. It always gets the discussion started."
Me: "Then when did you figure out it was me?"
Sister: "When you and Brenda got into it and she asked you
what your problem was with Yves Green."
Me: "Really?"
Sister: "Yep. It was the look in your eyes. Like you'd been
found out. That's when I knew. You were talking about him like
you knew him."

R

The Maas Point Resort is located on a small isthmus of land
just north of Vero Beach, Florida. It's got four pools and nine
tennis courts and a golf course and kayaks and a white sand

beach on the ocean side and fishing boats on the channel side. We decided to hold the EXPLODE weekend because several years ago a man approached me after one of Yves' talks and told me he owns resorts all over the country and if we ever wanted to rent one out for a big event, he'd be happy to see if he could help us out. I kept his card.

Y

It's a different sort of pit in the stomach. Yes, there are nerves, basic public speaking sort of nerves. They're there. I assume they'll always be there. But there's a calm there as well. Since leaving the H, I have thought about little else than this moment. I can't imagine the hours Rooster and Noll and Claudia have put into this. On top of the work they were already doing just to pull off the EXPLODE we'd been planning for months before I added my idea. I can't say I'm that concerned whether it "works" or not. Something died up on the mountain. Somebody died up on the mountain.

And someone else came back to life.

One more song, a little video, lights up, and I take the stage. It wasn't long ago I was a bearded man in group therapy, and now I'm a clean shaven motivational speaker about to address my most hard core fans.

I open my mouth. There is no turning back. "Welcome to Explode."

I have to wait for them to stop cheering and sit back down.

"All those months of planning and getting ready and anticipating and now we're here. On behalf of my staff and all of the people here at Maas Point, we welcome you and want you to know we're thrilled you could come. To begin with, how many of you have your cell phone on you?"

Every hand goes up.

"How many of you have both your cell phones on you?"

Laughter. Knowing looks. A shocking number of hands go up.

"And if you brought three or more cell phones with you, then you shouldn't be here!" They're loving it.

"Now if you could please pass your cell phones to the center aisles, we'll collect them and return them to you at the end of the weekend."

I knew they wouldn't know if I was being serious or not. They hesitate.

"Seriously. We'll take them. And laptops, too. Please pass them in to the center."

R

I'm standing in the back of the room in a cold sweat. He was supposed to come back from the desert less crazy, not more. Does he seriously think people are going to turn over their computers and phones? This opening part wasn't in our plan.

Y

They're starting to realize I'm serious. Time to amp things up.

"How many of you want to live on the edge? How many of you want to try something new? Is there anyone here who wants this weekend to be unlike any other?"
A few cheers. Keep it going.

"Well then, turn it over. The phone, the laptop, the tablet, turn'em over. You'll get them back. Maybe." A few laughs, good. The room is turning.

"You came to EXPLODE this weekend because you want to be stretched, you want to travel into the unknown, you want to take your game to a whole new level, right?"

R
Whatever he's doing here, it's working. They're starting to warm up. He is great at what he does. Crazy, but great.

Y
"Excellent. I see a pile of laptops forming at the end of that aisle. Nice, you're starting to get it!

This takes a while but eventually there are piles of gadgets in the aisles. I have no idea how we'll sort it out later, but Rooster will figure out.

R
Great. I guarantee he's assuming that I'll figure out a way to make sure everybody gets theirs back on Sunday.
And I will.

Y
"How many of you always have your cell phone on you? Every day? All day?"

Most of the hands go up.

"How many of you check your email more than once a day?"
Duh. Every hand goes up.

"How many of you check your email every hour?" Again,
almost every hand.
"How many of you, be honest, if you haven't checked your
email within two hours start to get a little tense?"

Slowly, hands go up.

"How many of you made more money last year than the year
before?"

Lots of hands go up.

"How many of you haven't taken a day off in the past week?"
Every hand.
"How many of you haven't taken a day off in the past month?"
Again, every hand, or close to it.

R
What is the point of this? I look over at Noll who's leaning
against the back wall next to Claudia. They both look back at
me, as if I know what Yves is up to here.

Y

"Okay, here's the thing. I'm so honored that you came and I
loved reading through your applications, but the truth is, you
don't need to work harder. And you don't need to be more
efficient or learn to multitask more. You don't need seven more
steps that will help you achieve more. You're already doing
great things in the world. So we're not going to spend one
minute this weekend trying to get better or bigger or faster or
stronger. I want to give you a gift. I'm prepared for some of you
—or maybe all of you—to not appreciate or understand this
gift. That's fine. And if, at the end of the weekend, you don't
want to keep the gift, I will refund you your registration. No
questions asked. Are we clear?"

It is silent. No one says anything. Nothing coming from the
crowd. I press on.

"Because it is possible, in our desire to be the best, to
achieve, to win, to accumulate, to build, to create—it is
possible that in our passionate pursuit of greatness, we may
miss what really matters. So here's what I want to do: I want to
hang out with you this weekend. That's it. I want us to eat and
laugh and tell stories and sit around and do nothing. Together.
I don't want us to accomplish one thing. I don't want us to
learn anything. I don't want you to get any more fired up than
you already are. I want us to simply be. Together. With each

other. And with some other people who will be joining us.
Now."

R

I nod to Noll who has already cued the resort manager. She in
turn gives the signal to her staff, who are each standing at one
of the sets of double doors along the south wall of room,
which opens up into the lobby.

They open the doors.

In the lobby are wives and husbands and children and friends
and partners who begin streaming through the doors, looking
for their dad or mom or partner or friend. At first the EXPLODE
attendees don't get it because it appears that random people
are crashing their exclusive time with Yves Green. But when
they start realizing it's the families of the people sitting around
them and they see kids jumping into their parents arms and
husbands and wives embracing, you can immediately see it
click on their faces: "Is my family surprising me, too? Did Yves
Green contact my family and arrange for them to surprise me
and stay with me—and did he pay for it?" So they start getting
up from their chairs and walking towards the mass of people
who are coming in to the room and they're searching and
looking and scanning the crowd and it's chaotic and emotional

and kids are yelling and laughing and climbing on chairs to get
a better view.

And Yves is standing there on stage taking it all in.

Y

They did it. Noll and Rooster and Claudia did it. We did it.

R

I decide that I am finally going to ask him. I can't endure
another day not knowing. I walk over to Noll, who is standing
in the back with his arm around Claudia.

Me: "Noll, I've wanted to ask you something for seven years.
And now that you were able to pull this off, I have to ask you:
What did you do between the time you left Vietnam and went
to work for Yves?"
Noll: "Why do you ask?"
Me: "Because you have all of these mysterious skills that you
picked up somewhere that allow you to do things that defy the
imagination—like locating the families of three hundred people
all around the country and making contact with them without
their father or mother or husband or wife knowing about it and
then getting them plane tickets and rides from the airport...it
makes my head spin. I've always assumed it was something

like the C.I.A. or the Secret Service. It had to be something top secret and covert and dangerous, right? Where did you learn to do things like this? What did you do before you came to work for Yves?" Noll smiles, plucks the end of his waxed mustache, and says, "Amway, Rooster, Amway."

Y

This is the best view in the room, up on the stage. I can see every one of the reunions. Every time a family finds each other I am moved. I can't get enough of it. I don't want it to end.

And now, yes, good, one last surprise. Although I had hoped for it. Standing in the doorway farthest from the stage I see a young woman, about high school age, and beside her the president of Big Girl Lemonade.

R

I am watching all of this and once again, I'm tearing up. Just a little. I realize in that moment that there is something I must do. I have been meaning to do this for a while, and now I decide that it's the time. Chuck Flannel said that I couldn't "make eyes" at her, but he didn't say I couldn't call her. I'm going to call her. I'm trembling at the thought. How does this woman reduce me to nerves like this? You know what it's going to take to call her? That's right, say it with me now: Millones de Delores Cojones.

books
plays
art
music
RobCast episodes
sessions under the trees in OJAI
robbell.com

Where'd You Park Your Spaceship goods
robbell.com